# VOICES

## Seymour Shubin

STEIN AND DAY/Publishers/New York

First published in 1985
Copyright © 1985 by Seymour Shubin
All rights reserved, Stein and Day, Incorporated
Designed by Terese Bulinkis Platten
Printed in the United States of America
STEIN AND DAY/*Publishers*
Scarborough House
Briarcliff Manor, NY 10510

**Library of Congress Cataloging-in-Publication Data**

Shubin, Seymour.
  Voices.

  I. Title.
PS3569.H754V6   1985        813'.54        84-40629
ISBN 0-8128-3002-4

To Sol Stein
for his faith and counsel

# Acknowledgment

I owe my son Neil a deep and loving debt of gratitude for his enthusiasm that helped get this book started, and for his insights and suggestions that helped shape it.

# VOICES

# VOICES

Also by Seymour Shubin

ANYONE'S MY NAME
MANTA
WELLVILLE, U.S.A.
HOLY SECRETS
THE CAPTAIN

# 1

---

HER EYES SPRANG open to the blackness of the night and the hammering of her heart. She started to sit up, to try to flee something, then sank back, aware with a great rush of relief that she was in bed. But she remained caught up in the nightmare, though she couldn't recall it, not a single part, not a face, nothing. She took a deep breath, let it out. She felt herself easing away from whatever she had dreamed. By now other thoughts were nipping at her.

Had to get two new tires—she'd meant to, but was so damn busy. And go over to the bank for a new supply of checks. And food shopping, she should go tonight. Rachel could do some of it after camp, of course—she often did—but there were certain things only she herself could do: many times she didn't know what she wanted until she saw it. Should go tonight, but had to send out more résumés, had to . . .

Wasn't this nonsense? Why did everything become such a big deal in the middle of the night?

Lynn felt herself growing calmer. But only for a few moments. Then—something that had been lurking behind all the other thoughts—it came out; filled her mind, as it had been doing more and more the past couple weeks.

How long could she keep lying? To her daughter. To everyone.

Her heart was pounding again. She felt herself breathing hard along the pillow.

She needed only a little more time!

But how much more time?

Just a little. Just a little.

Her heart, her breathing were slowing.

Just a little. Just—just a little.

SHE WOKE TO the distant sound of an alarm clock radio. A traffic report. She reached over and turned off her own alarm clock—Rachel had hers set a few minutes earlier. She remained in bed, listening to Rachel's footsteps as she padded into the bathroom, then to the flushing of the toilet, then to the rush of the shower. All that was left of the night was a faint uneasiness. And even that, as she swung her legs off the bed and slowly stood up, was fading.

Damn it, she knew what she was doing.

She lifted the blinds, and the early sun of a July morning brightened the room. It was so cool in the house—in fact, too cool, she should lower the air conditioner—that it was hard to believe it was supposed to be another scorcher today. She stood looking out the window, at the marigolds and geraniums near the hedge that separated her property from her neighbor to the left. The lawn, front and rear, was just about the right size: workable without a gardener. She should run the sprinkler this evening.

She went to the mirror and ran a comb through her hair. She fought a few little knots, then worked the comb easily down its auburn length. Actually, it was getting too long, a little longer than shoulder length, the way she liked it. And the past couple of months or so she'd become aware of a few filaments of gray. But it didn't bother her. Everyone in her family turned gray early—thirty-three was even late. Furthermore—and this was strange—she'd always liked white hair, even when she was a little girl, had promised herself that when she was old she'd never dye her hair. Maybe it was because she'd hated her own—she had been sure she would remain a carrot top and, worse, would always be called

12

Reds. Or maybe because Aunt Maryellen, her favorite aunt, may she rest in peace, had such beautiful white hair, while her mother, rest in peace, had kept dyeing hers a more and more atrocious red.

She heard Rachel coming out of the bathroom.

"Morning, Rachel." Lynn had come out into the hall.

"Morning." Rachel, wrapped in a pink towel, nodded as she walked toward her room, her little face—Lynn always thought of it as a baby face—in another towel, her hair glistening wet. Now would come a long session with the blower.

Lynn stepped into the stall shower in her own bathroom. As she adjusted the water, she thought about washing her hair, but decided to hold off until tonight, didn't want to spend time drying it. She wanted to make sure Rachel got a good breakfast—she'd been letting her get off with just a glass of milk, and once not even that, the past few days.

She raised her face to the water, trying to keep her hair away from it, then washed her face and let the water drain the soap away. As she soaped her full breasts, she instinctively was on the alert for lumps, and glanced routinely to make sure that the sprinkling of freckles across her shoulders and upper part of her breasts didn't suddenly hide any other kind of mark. If anything frightened her, that was it, and now she could relax and enjoy the shower. She soaped her belly, then her buttocks, her pubis, then down around her long legs.

You've got some "bod," Mom.

She got a big kick out of Rachel.

But she really was fortunate. For someone who enjoyed food, she was a nice weight for her height—at five-six, never more than a hundred and twenty. And her tummy was still pretty firm, her thighs firm and slender.

She dried herself vigorously, then hearing Rachel in the kitchen, threw on a thin robe and went downstairs. But Rachel, stuffing her polo shirt into her shorts—only the really little *kids,* she claimed, wore the day camp T-shirt—again only wanted milk.

"Come on, let me make you some French toast."

"No, I'm late. I'm going to miss the bus."

"You're not going to miss any bus. You've got a half hour."

But Rachel didn't seem to hear. She was standing by the refrigerator, sniffing at the snout of the carton of milk.

"Rachel, you nut, I just bought that yesterday. Look at the date."

"I hate sour milk."

"I just love it. I always buy sour milk."

"Moth-er!"

"Rach-el!"

Rachel eyed her as she brought the milk over to the table. She filled a glass.

"Lady," Lynn said, "I know I may be traumatizing you, I know you may end up spending years talking about this to a psychiatrist, but you've got to start having breakfast."

Rachel drained half a glass. Lynn watched her. It was like looking at herself at that age. A human motor that could talk every minute of the day.

"Do you promise me you'll eat lunch?"

"Yup," she said between gulps of milk.

"I'm not sure what you said. Yup or yep?"

"Yup." She tilted her head back to finish it.

"Will you slow up? *Please?*"

Rachel set down the empty glass, then slumped back.

"You're going to have an ulcer by twelve."

"I am twelve."

"Really now. It's not over yet."

Rachel sat for maybe a half a minute, then came over and kissed her and started to dart off—several kids in the neighborhood went to the same camp, and there was a lot to talk about at the bus stop. Lynn grabbed her arm, looked at her with a smile. Rachel released a breath; she seemed to go limp, slowly. Then she smiled. She sat on Lynn's lap and hugged her hard.

"I—can't breathe," Lynn groaned. It was an old game. It meant: squeeze harder. Rachel obliged. "You're going to be late," Lynn joked.

"Moth-er." This time it was a deliberate affectation.

"Rach-el."

Lynn squeezed her. They'd always been very close, even before Jon took off.

14

Rachel jumped up again. Except for her hair—blonde, almost like Jon's—she was almost her image. Same big green eyes. Same triangular face, with a slight hollow at the cheeks. Tall, but not too tall—about Lynn's height at her age. Slender. And the smile—both of them had a way of talking with a little smile.

"Bye." Rachel kissed her forehead quickly, then hurried toward the door.

"See you. Have a good day."

"Bye."

Once the door closed, the apartment went instantly hushed. It was a lonely kind of silence. Lynn stared at the door.

How could Jon do this to Rachel? Not call or write for months at a time? Let months go by without sending her a cent?

Such a great kid. A great, great kid.

She would kill for her. Honest to God.

LYNN SAT AT the table a while longer, not aware she was simply staring, then gathered up a few dishes and put them in the dishwasher. She felt very tired all at once, wished she could go back to bed. At the same time she wanted to get away from the silence.

All of the anxieties of the night had come back.

Just a few weeks more of the lie, no matter what. Three weeks. Three. Two, maybe, but three at the most.

She washed her face again in the bathroom, more to clear her head than anything else, and went into her bedroom to finish dressing. She decided on a different skirt than the one she'd set out, and a blouse she'd almost forgotten she had. As she started for the door, she remembered that she wanted to keep a spare umbrella in the office. She got it from the hall closet.

Driving her three-year-old Volvo out of the garage, she remembered about the tires. On her way home she would stop at that place down the street. Yesterday she'd called several places, and though tires were like Latin to her, this place, as far as she could make out, had given her the best price.

What a gorgeous morning. It was almost springlike, though they predicted it would hit ninety by noon. Of all the seasons, she loved the summer best. No—not really true. Actually she loved all the seasons—liked the beach, liked to ski, liked snow at Christmas, a fireplace. It was one of the reasons she and Jon had decided to stay in Maryland, though he'd gotten an excellent offer to go with a firm in Los Angeles if he'd take the bar there. In fact, the reason they'd picked this house over two others—each of them just about the same commute to Baltimore, where he had his office—was the fireplace.

Funny, she almost did it again.

She had just passed an intersection where, for the past eight years, she would make a left that would take her to Crain & Crain Chemicals. And though it was six months now, sometimes—like an old horse sensing the barn—she would still nearly make that turn.

She'd worked four years in the secretarial pool, then three as an executive secretary in the promotion department, and finally as one of the copywriters. Then one afternoon as she was working on a brochure, her boss, with his stonelike bald head, peered into her L-unit. "Lynn, can I see you in my office?"

And there: "Lynn, I'm terribly sorry, but it's bad news." The company was cutting back, about a hundred people were being laid off, and because she was the last one hired in the department—what could he say? "I can't tell you how sorry I am. You know what I think of your work."

True. He'd been so impressed by letters she'd composed for him as his secretary that he had suggested she try out as a writer. Still, a job she loved suddenly gone. And an excellent salary gone. And Rachel to support.

She said desperately, "Do you know if there's anything else in the company?"

"Lynn, they're cutting down everywhere. Even secretaries. But, look, you shouldn't have any trouble finding something. You're good. And you know the recommendation I'll give you."

So, after eight years, out of there with three weeks' pay and no more Blue Cross/Blue Shield (you had to be there nine years to be vested) and unemployment checks. And after some seventy-five résumés, six employment agencies and many interviews, she

16

still hadn't found anything as a copywriter, or even a secretarial job that would come close to supporting them.

About fifteen miles from her home she turned onto a busy, commercial avenue that soon entered an area of widely scattered shops and old Victorian buildings that had been converted into offices. She turned into a driveway leading up to one of the buildings. The wooden Colonial sign hanging from a post on the lawn listed two companies. One was Thomas Hadley, CPA. Underneath that was Master Surveys, Inc.

She parked among a cluster of cars, sat for a little while with the motor off. Then she drew in a breath and walked up the wooden steps to the open porch. She opened the door to a pleasant rush of cool air. Inside, on the first floor, she could see Thomas Hadley in his office, working at what she knew to be a calculator: he was always at the calculator. She walked up to the second floor. The reception room was furnished in Danish modern; abstract paintings were on the beige walls. Tina, skinny, middle-aged, with a chalk white face beneath scraggly black bangs, was at the telephone console. Tina fluttered a hand at her, then had to go back to the phones.

Lynn went to the farthest office and closed the door. It was a small office, tastefully furnished and softly lighted. The desk was uncluttered; it seemed to exist only to hold a phone. A light on the phone immediately went on, but she took her time answering. She adjusted the venetian blinds several times before she was satisfied. She looked in her handbag for a tissue and dabbed at her nose, sniffing. A half dozen doctors had told her she didn't have a deviated septum or a sinus problem or allergies; still one nostril occasionally closed up.

She sat in a soft chair by the desk. She toe-ed off each shoe.

Oh, Jesus. So hard, it was always so hard to start.

She picked up the phone. There was a little beating at the base of her throat. It was spreading throughout her chest.

"Hi," Tina said. "Comfy?"

"Comfy cozy."

"I love your skirt. That's your color. Have you had coffee?"

"Yes. At home."

"You have a cold?"

"No. Hold on a second." She blew her nose again. "No, I'm fine now."

"Okay," Tina said in a singsong way. "Buckle up. It's Terry Green."

He came on. "Hello?"

"Hi."

"Hello? This you, Dawn?"

"Hi there."

A pause.

Let's pretend, he said, that she was lying naked on a beach.

# 2

THE STUDENT NURSE suddenly wanted to run out of the room. She had brought in a new delivery of flowers, thinking she would just set them down on the windowsill and leave; or maybe, if Mrs. Radcliff was awake, would give her the cards or read them to her. But she hadn't expected this, the crying. Mrs. Radcliff, her hands on Mr. Owens's arms, was sobbing as he was trying to comfort her.

"Try to think," he was saying softly, "that the important thing you've lost is your cancer. Try to think of it that way. 'I've lost my cancer.'"

Yes, the student nurse thought, and two breasts. What could a man, even if he was a nurse, and even if he was as nice as Mr. Owens, what could he really know what it was like to lose two breasts? *Breasts.* Just thinking of it did little things to her heart and stomach, especially since Mrs. Radcliff wasn't all that much older, only ten years.

She set down the flowers and, with a slight feeling of guilt that she only wanted to leave, left.

"I'm sorry," Mrs. Radcliff was saying to Mr. Owens.

"Sorry? Why should you be sorry?" He looked at her with a

19

smile. "You're afraid your husband'll come in and find you in someone else's arms?"

"Yeah." She wiped at her eyes and settled back. She looked at him, breathing hard. "It was a good cry, though. I don't remember the last time I cried like that. Hysterical, yes, I've been hysterical. But just a good cry . . ." She wiped her eyes again.

He said nothing. Just kept his hand on her arm.

She said, "Why did I cry with you?"

"Oh, maybe I've just got a sad face."

"That's not true. Can I say something to you?"

"I think you know you can."

"When I first came in and saw—a man—a man, a nurse—I was a little uneasy. I felt I wouldn't be able to really talk— Or—I don't know. Just that it wouldn't be as good. But—you're really something. Do you mind my saying it?"

"That I'm something?"

She smiled and squeezed his hand. He rose up from the bed. "Look, don't be so slow about using the buzzer."

"I just hate being a nuisance."

"Come on. That's silly. You're spoiling us."

She smiled. "Thanks."

"I'll be back soon."

He walked back to the nursing station and sat down heavily. He reached for one of the charts and opened it, just to do something. His hands, suddenly, were almost trembling.

It wasn't just Mrs. Radcliff, so anguished; it had just become hard, almost unbearable, to take suffering any more—the teenager in 324 who'd lost a leg in a car accident, the woman in 325 with lung cancer, crying that she'd never smoked; even the minor things—the gall bladder in 326, the appendectomy in 320 . . .

"Leon, you on tomorrow?" It was Maggie, one of the other nurses.

"Yes."

"What made me think you weren't?" she said, frowning; she'd already started walking away.

"Maybe you know something I don't," he called after her lightly.

20

He smiled as she turned. She said, "I don't know where I got that."

He returned to the chart. The smile was quivering on his lips. Couldn't any of them tell? Couldn't they see how he was fighting to hold himself together? It had been going on for at least a year, when Della first started threatening to leave; probably even before that—the feeling that he couldn't look at another dying person, another wound, hear another cry.

Burnout. They called it burnout. They even had support groups for nurses, and he'd gone to a couple of the sessions. He'd even said something about himself, how sometimes he dreaded walking into the hospital. And several of them spoke up in agreement—that's the way they sometimes felt too, so don't feel you're unusual. It's only when you feel that way most of the time, or it affects your work, that it's a real problem. Get a hobby, they'd said; exercise; take long walks in the country; go on vacation; be aware of flowers, the colors of the sky; *revive* yourself.

They made it sound so simple.

He'd been afraid to tell them he *did* feel that way most of the time, and about the hundred other things that were eating at him. Being a man in a woman's field. Patients assuming you're a doctor or an orderly because you're a man. People thinking you must be a fag. And about Della and her not letting him see the boy. Had been afraid to tell them because they might say look for another kind of work—and what kind of work could he do after sixteen years?

He kept looking at the chart.

Sometimes he had the frightening ability to stand as though at a distance and look at himself. These were generally times when he was pretending, was acting in a different way from how he felt. Like now. He could see himself the way others must see him, a man in his late thirties, with round bright cheeks and short blond hair, with muscular forearms showing under his short-sleeved white jacket, and with the narrow name tag L. OWENS RN over his left chest. They saw him looking so absorbed, and now standing up and putting away the chart and going into another patient's room, this time to take a blood pressure.

When he came out, he looked at his watch. He felt a surge of anxiety. It was twenty to twelve. Twenty more minutes.

Should he? Shouldn't he?

Shouldn't. Mustn't.

Especially here.

Now, at lunch break, he walked down the corridor, telling himself he really wasn't going to do it. But as he approached one of the offices toward the end of the corridor, his hand went into his pocket and felt around for a key.

It wasn't only wrong, it was crazy.

But he took out the key. Darkness lay behind the frosted glass; the surgeon was on vacation. After a fast glance around, he turned the lock quickly, stepped in and closed the door, pushing in the locking button on the knob. He sagged against the wall, away from the door, and waited for his heart to stop booming. It wouldn't stop.

It was safe, he assured himself. After all, he was the only nurse on the floor, this shift, who had the key; one nurse each shift had to have it in case of an emergency.

Safe, but not completely safe. Administration probably had one. But they wouldn't just come into a dark office, would they?

He went over to the desk and sat down and put his hand on the phone. Then he lifted it quickly, got an outside line and began dialing.

Softly, "Let me talk to Dawn. This is Wing."

"Just a moment, please."

There was still time to hang up, he could still—

"Hi there."

"Dawn?"

"Hi. How are you today?"

"Okay." His throat felt closed. He looked at the door.

She said, "I can barely hear you."

"Now?"

"That's a little better." Then, "The last time I talked to you, you had a cold. How is it?"

That was a couple days ago—it felt so good she remembered. "No, I'm fine."

"Oh, that's good. Summer colds are *the* worst. So, is anything new in your life? Anything exciting?"

"No. Except I've been looking forward to talking to you."

"Have you? That's so nice. I've been thinking about you too."

"What've you been thinking?"

"Oh, lots of—"

Oh no! A shadow had suddenly formed on the glass. He started to hang up, but knew that wouldn't do any good. He sat frozen. It was a back—a man was standing with his back to the door.

He had begun to turn, the shadow revolving slowly into profile.

Leon half rose, but now the shadow was joined by another. They blended together and then gradually moved away.

He sank back on the chair. He lifted the receiver, but could hardly breathe. "Dawn?"

"What happened?"

"Nothing. Hold on." He kept breathing through his mouth. "I'm sorry."

"What's wrong?"

"Nothing . . . Dawn?" This was crazy . . . "You there?"

"I'm right here."

His eyes stayed on the door. "You said you were thinking of me. What were you thinking?"

"Oh, lots of good things. When will Wing be calling again."

"You really mean that?"

"I wouldn't say it. I don't have to say it. You sound like such a very gentle person. Yet a strong person. Of course I think about you."

He put his mouth closer to the mouthpiece. "Dawn?"

"Yes, honey, I'm right here with you."

"Could you? Would you? Please?"

"Would I what, sweetheart?"

"You know. What I asked. Meet me?"

"Wing, I really can't. I told you. I'm not allowed. They won't let me. It's against the rules."

"Please? I'll give you anything. I've got money. I'll even mail it. I trust you. I trust you to show up."

"No, honey, I really can't. I'd lose my job."

"I'll give you money. I'll give you—You just name it—Any-thing . . ."

"Oh, honey, that's so sweet. But I can't. Can't we just talk?"

He closed his eyes, took a deep breath.

She said, "You there?"

He took another breath. "Dawn. Dawn, I want you."

"Oh, honey, that's so sweet. How do you want me?"

"I—I want everything. I want to be there. I want to be with you."

"We are together, honey, you're right here."

"Dawn? Tell me. What're you wearing?"

"Oh, what do you see me wearing?"

"I don't know. A negligee—A little sweater, a skirt. High heels . . . Dawn? I'd like to put my hand up your skirt. I want to feel you. I want to feel you naked."

"Tell me what you're feeling."

"Your—behind. Your beautiful ass. And your breasts. I want to kiss your breasts . . . bite them . . ."

"But not hard, please not hard."

"No, not hard . . ."

"You're always so gentle."

She did remember! "Dawn?"

"Yes, sweetheart."

"I've—I've just taken it out."

"Is it big? Big and hard?"

"Yes. It's so big . . . Dawn?"

"Yes, honey."

"Do it to yourself. Please do it, Dawn."

"I will, honey." Her voice changed slightly, became softer, as though she were afraid someone might overhear.

"You won't. I know you won't."

"Hon-ey, I thought you knew me. You still don't know me very well."

"You won't. I know. And I can't, I don't want to, unless . . ."

"Hon-ey, I will."

"Swear to me," he whispered fiercely.

"I swear. I will. But don't rush me. You never rush me. That's why I can with you, why I want to with you. I can't get ready that fast. Just let me lie back . . ."

24

"Are you lying back?"

"Yes."

"Are your legs open?"

"Oh, yes."

"Are you? Are you doing it yet?"

"Not yet. Hold on, just—There. Yes."

"Are you?"

"Yes." Her voice had become fainter. "Oh, yes."

"You're not."

"Don't say that. Please. Just do it . . . Are you?"

"Yes. Tell me. What're you doing? Is your finger in there?"

"Oh my, yes. I've got it in there."

"Where is it?"

"It's in my pussy. Oh, it's deep in my pussy."

"Are you wet yet?"

"Oh, honey, I'm so wet. So wet." She seemed to be trying to catch her breath. "Oh, honey, I'm so wet. I can't keep my pussy still."

"Let me put it in you. I want—Spread your legs—Let me—I want to be in you."

"Yes. Yes. Please."

"I'm putting it in you. Do you feel me?"

"Yes. Put it in deep. Deep. Deeper. Yes. Give it to me. Give it to me good, give it to me hard."

"I'm giving it to you, honey. Oh, I'm giving it to you. Do you feel me?"

"Oh, do I feel you. So good. So strong. Deeper. Deeper."

"Tell me when you're going to come. Tell me."

"Soon. Soon. Not yet, but soon."

"Tell me. Tell me when."

"Soon. Any second. Are you?"

"Not yet."

"Oh, you're too much, it's too much, I can't take it."

"Are you coming?"

"It's too much, you're too much—Any second. Are you? . . . Yes. It's starting. It's going to—Are you?"

"Yes."

"Oh, honey." Her breathing had become gasps. "Oh, honey, you're so good. It's so good."

25

"Oh, Dawn. Dawn."

Don't end, please never end, never, never . . .

But gradually, gradually ending. And ended.

LYNN WAS FINISHED at five, her place taken by a young woman, no more than nineteen, who attended community college during the day. Manya, who was manager, and Louise were touching up their hair in front of the reception room mirror when she came out; another woman had replaced Tina at the telephone console. Manya, a tiny, honeycombed-blonde in her forties, said, "I was saying. My daughter brought her kid over, they both got these damn summer colds, it's going around. The last thing I need."

"Do you take vitamins?" Louise asked.

"God, I ran out two months ago. I keep telling myself—"

"You should take vitamins. . . . Lemme help you." Lynn's blouse had twisted in back around her belt. Louise, who one of the women said had been a hooker in her younger days, was about fifty—she was pillowed with fat, and wore rings on almost every finger but her thumbs. "Wait, there's a thread caught."

Lynn felt Louise's hand working, then the blouse came loose. She slipped it into her skirt, adjusting it.

Louise said, "I had another guy wanted his wife to listen in." She pretended to gag. Then she continued fixing her hair. They generally didn't talk about the calls, only the most unusual ones. Apparently she had said what she'd had to, and that was enough.

Walking down the stairs to the first floor, Manya said, "Do you know where Sam and I had a great meal? Hills. You ever been there?"

"You like Hills?" Louise said. "The last two times, I thought just fair."

"Really?"

Thomas Hadley was standing in his office with his wife. Louise called, "Good night."

Both Hadleys turned and waved. "Good night. Night."

Manya's husband, a cigar centered in his mouth, was standing next to his car. He walked around and opened the door for her. "Good night," she said.

"Good night."

26

"Night." Then Louise, as they walked to their cars, said, "I—am—tired. I use my mouth all day, but my feet get tired."

Lynn laughed. In the car, she started the motor and air conditioner, then sat for a while, feeling the stirring of anxiety. Generally, the only times during the day she felt caught up in anxiety about what she was doing was coming in in the morning and going home—leaving that other world and then going back to it, to Rachel, who thought she spent the day doing telephone surveys of products and whatever. But Lynn knew she must be tense throughout the day, though she was usually too busy to think much about it. As with Louise and her feet, she usually ended up with aching muscles in her arms and calves.

She wondered as she drove off if she should go shopping before dinner or afterward. She decided on afterward—then thought maybe she would hold off until tomorrow. She would go out with Rachel for dinner—she wasn't up to cooking, and hadn't asked Rachel to prepare anything.

It really felt as if she'd been doing this longer than eight weeks. (Or was it nine? No, eight.) Maybe it was because she tended to mix up the interview with the actual day she started. The interview had been two weeks earlier. There'd been a simple little ad in the classified section of the paper—something about a woman wanted, with a good telephone voice. And when she'd met Thomas Hadley and his wife, Mary, she had naturally assumed they wanted a receptionist. But it took forever for Thomas Hadley—who did just about all of the talking—to get around to it. He simply seemed eager to take some time off and talk. A pleasant enough fellow, balding, about forty-one or -two, with a bow tie and jacket. Liked to talk, most of the time, with his hands locked behind his head, chair tilted back.

What do you do? Any children? That's a . . . Massachusetts accent, isn't it? Boston? Thought so. How long've you been living here? Worked at Crain & Crain? He knew someone who worked at Crain & Crain—no, that was Quinson & Quinson. Crain & Crain. Quinson & Quinson—he made a face, annoyed he'd mixed them up.

"Early senility," he said, smiling. And, with those hands behind his head, he went on, this time about himself. He had a good, basically one-man accounting practice, which meant he was out servicing accounts a good part of the time. He had a full-time secretary, but his wife came in to help out, as did his father, who'd been a bookkeeper as far back as his days in the old country, Czechoslovakia. He also had some real estate holdings, which he ran from here, and an interest in an orthopedic supply company, and owned the business upstairs, Master Surveys.

"Now." He unclasped his hands and folded his arms on his chest. "The job is in Master Surveys. Actually, a branch of it. Called Phone Friend."

Master Surveys, a marketing research service, had just two employees, his sister and sister-in-law. "A bit of nepotism," he smiled. "Phone Friend, at the present time we employ nine women. Some part-time. If you're at all interested in the position, I'd like you to talk to some of them. We have housewives, we have some college students, we have two young women who're artists—you know, it's hard making a living out of art—we also have a ballerina, a very, very fine young woman. In fact, Mary works there part-time."

Mary Hadley, a chunky little woman wearing a wide-brimmed hat, smiled but said nothing. She stood leaning against the windowsill.

Had you, he asked after a pause, ever heard of "sexual telephone consultations?"

She stared at him, not sure what he meant. Then she recalled seeing some ads in one of the men's magazines. . . . Was this—this guy and his wife for real? With no change of expression, he was going through some papers on his desk. Then he showed her a photocopy of a small classified ad.

"We run this in various papers and men's magazines. We get calls from throughout the country."

It read: *Phone Friend: Fantasies, life problems, dreams explored. No restrictions.* And it listed a phone number.

"We talk about anything they want to talk about. We also help them, if they want, to act out their sexual fantasies. Most, I should add, do."

What *bullshit.* And he was so goddam *serious.* She wanted to laugh, but it would have been a nervous laugh.

28

If she was worried about the legality, he was saying, there was nothing to worry about. "I've been in this business four years. I was in court once—that was the third week we opened—and it was thrown out. And if there are any other legal hassles, it would involve me, not you." As for the customers, there would be nothing for her to worry about either. She'd never see them, they'd never see her. The phone was just a number to them; it wasn't listed anywhere with an address. Callers used credit cards. And all the calls were screened by their operator. The only things to avoid were pretending you were a licensed psychotherapist, and talking to anyone who sounded like he might be under twenty-one—whenever in doubt, don't.

"Thanks," she said with a shake of her head, "but no thanks. I'm afraid I don't have the imagination."

"You really don't need all that much of an imagination." He smiled. "It's all down on file cards, really, if you need help. And my manager will help you. She's got enough imagination for twelve people. Mrs. Kallen. A very lovely person. I'm sure you'd like her."

"I'm sure I would." But no. She smiled and shook her head again.

"If I may say something," Mary Hadley spoke up. "We're open from nine A.M. to two A.M. You can pretty much work the hours you want."

"That's right," he said. "And one of these days we'll be going twenty-four hours. All you have to do is let us know in advance what hours you want—say, two days in advance. You want to work a twenty-hour week? Four five-hour days? Two eight-hour days, one four-hour day? You want to work more—a forty hour week? Thirty hours? And now the bottom line. You get a commission on each call—we charge them forty-eight fifty a call. And I can show you my books, you can make a lot of money. An awful lot of money."

She shook her head again and stood up. He stood up with her, while Mrs. Hadley remained against the windowsill. "If you change your mind, call me. I love Boston accents."

Mrs. Hadley simply smiled goodbye.

Although Lynn thought she would look back on it as—well, a funny incident, something she couldn't wait to tell her friends, she'd found by the time she came home that it upset her. She really didn't want to think about it, let alone talk about it. It wasn't that it shocked her. What was sickening was that after eight years at one job, and years before that at other jobs, and after months of pounding the streets, this would pay so much more than anything she could find. And there was her anger at Jon, and her worry that she would have to give up the house—the mortgage payments were high, it was expensive to run. She couldn't even afford the area any more, and that would mean taking Rachel out of her old school, away from her friends.

She mustn't do that to her, had to find a way.

It was like when she was a kid, she'd thought that night, the only Gold in a South Boston neighborhood and a parochial school full of Kelleys and Learys, who only knew to call her kike when they got angry, even though she was Catholic and her mother was named Sweeney. It hadn't taken great brains to find the answer, just determination to use her teeth and fists and even, once, a full brick in the palm of her hand. Or finding the courage to go on to college, the only one in her family and among her friends who did; and finding the jobs to pay her way and give money at home, though she was to drop out after a year because, by then, Jon had proposed to her and she was determined to help put him through law school.

From her father—a carpet salesman, mostly, when he wasn't on a binge, and a frustrated standup comic—she'd gotten a sense of humor that could be, or at least used to be, a bit crazy. From her mother, a cocktail waitress who survived lung cancer (only to die at seventy after being hit by a kid on a ten-speed bike), two stillbirths and early widowhood, she was sure she got most of her strength. And from Jon?

If anything had really prepared her to do this sort of thing, it was their marriage. She'd never been uptight about *words*. Christ, she'd grown up with all the words—fuck, shit, and up yours went right along with blind man's buff and even jacks. And even if she hadn't, the one thing, one of the many things, she and Jon did have was the ability to say just about anything in their lovemaking. Maybe it was his playwright's mind, or maybe simply his need, but he would encourage her to join him in his fantasies, to say whatever he wanted, whatever she wanted.

30

It amazed her, the night she'd met the Hadleys, that—even though, oh Christ, it was completely out of the question—that she could even *think* of the possibility of calling Hadley.

But by the end of a couple of weeks, as she sat dialing his number, she'd become frustrated enough and determined enough to worry he wouldn't need her any more. And two days later she was turned over to Manya Kallen for training.

THIS SERVICE, MANYA had said, was a lot different from most of the other phone services throughout the country. "From what I hear about them, most give the customer maybe seven to ten minutes—the quicker the call, of course, the more the calls. We give them all the time they want. First, it shows we're really interested in them. Second," and here she smiled, "most are only going to take seven, ten minutes, two minutes, anyway. But it does show them," she said, her face serious again, "that we're not here just to— We're here to explore their fantasies, discuss whatever they want."

At a lot of other services too the calls came into a central answering service, and the operator had women return the calls from their homes. Too loose a system for Mr. Hadley; not businesslike enough. And also, of course, you couldn't compare this service with those telephone recording things, where even kids could call. *Kids.*

Manya, sitting behind her desk, shook her head disgustedly as Lynn looked at her in wonder. How do you—fool yourself this way?

"We get calls from all sorts of people—even some women. But we don't handle women. We get doctors, lawyers, ministers, psychiatrists, all sorts. Celebrities, you'd be surprised at some of the celebrities. When you're here a little while I'll show you some names, you wouldn't believe the names. I used to wonder, why do they give their names? I don't mean just the celebrities—"

"That's something I can't understand."

"Honey, let me tell you. For one thing, it's word of mouth—people know we can be trusted. I understand there are some services, maybe a lot of them, that sell the names. Not us. And we really help people. There are an awful lot of people—honey, there's so many people it'll make you want to cry—who're simply desperate, who need help. They don't want to go to a psychiatrist, they don't want to go to their minister, they don't want to go to a whore. They don't want to get caught, they're afraid they'll get herpes, they don't want to play around and louse up their marriage. There's a need, honey. We fill a big, big need. I look myself square in the face in the mirror. And I got a husband, I got a Sam, who wouldn't let me do it for two seconds if he thought it was like—you know, like I was whoring."

Oh bullshit, Lynn thought. The money.

"Not that we don't get the sickies. But sickies need help too." Manya, a bony, still vaguely attractive woman whose salmon-colored slacks were belted high on her slightly protruding belly, leaned back in her chair. "Do you have any questions so far?"

"Not yet." This was absolute madness . . .

"Okay. So let's go into some details, let's make believe there's a call. Oh. First. A name. You want to use Lynn?"

"No." With a shake of her head.

"Okay, so you'll think of a name. But I don't want any Honeys or Angels, nothing phony like that."

Absolute madness. She nodded.

"All right, our operator tells you there's a call. Joe Shmo. You never talked to him before, you don't know anything about him, he doesn't know anything about you. Okay? Now, the first thing to remember is this. Every person you talk to you've got to make feel special. I can't emphasize it enough. Special. Is important to you. Special. A special person. Okay?"

Special. Okay.

"Now one of the first things you'll hear—you'll hear it over and over—'I never did this before.' So he's telling you what? He's embarrassed. You've got to relax him. so you tell him, 'Just relax, there's nothing to be embarrassed about. Psychologists call me, psychiatrists call me, I get calls from rabbis, ministers.' And it's true. I've gotten calls from everyone. And if anyone asks you why a psychologist would call you, tell him what psychologists tell me, 'You know more about sex in a practical way than I do.' Okay?"

Manya was waiting, so she nodded.

"Sometimes they'll tell you they feel guilty or stupid or what-

32

ever. You tell them, 'What's there to feel guilty about? I don't understand.' In other words, make them feel foolish for feeling guilty—you know, it's only a *phone*. But these are just suggestions, you'll think of things. All right?"

She nodded again.

"All right, somewhere along the line he's going to ask what you look like. What do you say?"

Lynn thought. "I've got reddish hair, I—"

Wrong, wrong. Manya waved for her to stop. "What if it happens he doesn't like red hair? No offense—it might be he doesn't like blondes or brunettes. Whatever. No, you say something like, 'What do you think I look like?' If he says I think you're a tall blonde, chances are he likes tall blondes. Or if he says he doesn't know, he can't even guess, then you tell him whatever you want. You never get in any trouble saying you've got big breasts. Or tits—you can't ever go wrong with tits. Now, you don't waste too much time on this, understand. Otherwise you'll be talking an hour till you find out what they like. The point is, like I said, we're not like a lot of other services—bing, bang, hang up. We try to learn what their fantasies are."

"If they ask where I am?"

"In bed, at home. Where else? They'll say, 'What're you wearing?' Oh, a thin little thing, nothing underneath. All right, now he's back to 'I never did this before,' and he wants to know where to start, what to do. You say—you'll make up your own words after a while, it'll come natural—you say something like, 'What would you like to do? What have you always wanted to do?' And it generally comes out. If it doesn't, you might ask would he like you to do this to him, that to him, whatever. And you're passionate— okay, hot. You haven't had a cold day in your life. Now, ten out of ten—some days maybe eight out of ten, but most days ten out of ten—they'll want you to promise, to swear, you're doing just what they're doing, and that you're getting your—satisfaction. I swear to them on everything, but I try not to say 'honest to God.' I believe in honest to God—you're going to die if you lie. So, I swear to it any way else I can. And they not only want to make sure you're doing it, they want a complete description. And they want to *hear* it. Gasps. Moans. Okay? Do I have to paint pictures?"

"No, you already have."

"Okay." Manya took out a box of file cards from the bottom drawer of her desk. She began to flip through them, then stopped. "Before I forget. I don't have to tell you, you don't date any of the clients."

"No," Lynn said softly, "you don't have to tell me." In fact, the odds were she would be pulling out. No way could she handle this.

"I mean, some of these men, they can get to you. They'll plead, they'll beg, they'll offer diamonds. You hear this nice voice, and you think—"

"Manya, please. You don't have to tell me."

So look here, Manya said. These cards. "You probably won't need them after a while. But sometimes toward the end of the day, or maybe you're not feeling well, or you're really up to here with it, you can't think of a thing. Just go through these. There's every word in the book, every position, every situation. And, see, they've got headings and they're filed in alphabetical order."

Lynn ran her forefinger along them, stopping now and then. Yes, everything you ever wanted to know, or maybe never believed. Even where to moan. And written in compressed scripts.

"And of course you got me," Manya said. "I don't know how I came to be gifted, but I got a good imagination—in fact, I wrote most of the cards."

Lynn felt obligated to look at them again. Manya said, "Would you like to sit in on a couple of my calls?"

"No, no. That's not necessary."

"It's really not. Very easy to pick up. Did you ever do any acting?"

"In high school. Two plays."

"All it takes is acting. I've got a feeling you'll do fine. You've got a beautiful voice. And"—Manya looked at her with a little smile—"you've got something in your eyes. I call it 'doers' eyes.' Things don't throw you. You'll do whatever you have to do."

This was strange. Her mother called them "devil's eyes"—the first time was when she was suspended from elementary school for climbing out on a windowsill on a dare.

"So," Manya said. "Any questions?"

"Not that I can think of."

"Oh, there's something I forgot. Try to remember to keep some notes on each call, what he likes, what his problem is. So, if he calls back it's like you remember."

"All right."

But her voice had gone so flat, she was so sure she would never be back, that Manya apparently sensed it.

"Let me tell you something," Manya said. "First of all, it's just you, the phone and no one you're ever going to see in your life. Nobody here can even hear a word you're saying, unless you leave the door open or scream. Okay? Now let me tell you about me. You know something? When I leave this building I can't say the word shit. Can you believe that? It's true. Oh, I'll say it, it's not like I can't ever say it. That would be a lie. But I find the word sticks in my throat. But here? Here—"

Manya was looking at her, as though readying her for something.

"—I have no problem with pussy, cunt, shit, prick, fuck, suck, wet pussy, give it to me, I'm coming. I can do ooh, aah—you'd think my bellybutton would fly off. But they're just—words, sounds. They mean something to that person out there, but not to me. But when I go out of here and say shit, I really mean it, and I don't like the word. Does that make any sense?"

"I can understand it." Funny how she was getting to like this little lady.

"So—tomorrow?"

"Tomorrow." But still doubted it, though not as strongly.

And did of course come back, very nervous, very worried, her voice cracking those first few calls; and though it was the last thing she was concerned about, she couldn't help wondering why, since she was always alone in the room, they trusted her with the calls. It wasn't until two days later that Manya, after giving her a big hug, said, "I hope you don't mind, I can tell you now, but I listened in on the first five calls."

# 3

LEON PULLED INTO the driveway of his small, semidetached house. He entered through the back door and immediately took off the top of his nurse's uniform. Harry, an old alley cat he'd recently adopted, slithered toward him. He knelt down and stroked it, then went upstairs.

The house was so lonely, still. The house Della had left. Taking the boy.

He sat down on the side of the bed. He felt slightly sick to his stomach, had felt it ever since the call. But he'd known it would happen—just as he had always known years ago, on the way up to the bathroom or the attic, that he was going to suffer later, that even though no one living would be able to see him do it, God and all the dead were looking down.

Please, God, he'd pray afterward, don't let me do it again. Please, dear Jesus, help me, help me. And then he'd be so confident. But a couple of days later, or even the *same* day—something would start it again, maybe just an ad showing a woman in a bra, or thinking of someone like Mrs. Weinberg, who ran the grocery store—so homely, but he'd think of her taking him by the hand and leading him into a back room.

"There." That was the minister's word for it, Reverend Campbell, who maybe once a year would take a group of boys aside and warn them against touching "there." Sin. Weakens. Ruins your life. Or the way the guys in school, way back in the sixth grade even, what they'd do if they wanted to taunt you—making those jerk-off motions in the air, or grabbing your hand and twisting the palm up—"Hey, he's got hair!"

And now at his age, again, a grown man nearing his forties, even balding a little. And though he didn't believe any more that God—if there was a God—could see you in the smallest closet; that the dead—his father, all his uncles, his aunts—could see you too, yet it wouldn't go away, that the sky was filled with faces.

He had started making the calls out of curiosity. Someone—it was only two or three weeks before Della left—had given the number to him, but he hadn't really believed what it was and he'd called simply to find out. But when he had learned it was true, and the woman who answered asked did he have a credit card, he quickly hung up. Then over the next few days he called at least two more times, just to ask them about the service again, knowing he wasn't going through with it; just hearing some woman talking about it was a thrill.

Then he'd come up with the idea. He would never use a credit card, even if he had one; would never give his name, tell them anything about himself. So he'd asked if he could send them cash, with a name, and they'd given him a P.O. box number.

Wing would be calling.

He hadn't thought of it being so close to that chink's name. If he had he wouldn't have used it. Wang, Dr. Wang. A chink doctor at the hospital where Della worked as head nurse of the coronary care unit. Her boyfriend.

He lay back on the unmade bed and stared at the ceiling. Harry leaped up, startling him. He flung the cat aside, angry, but Harry crept back to him. His hand began stroking it slowly, then closed gently on its head. It felt fragile; he pictured it crumbling if he closed his fingers hard enough.

The phone rang. He was sure it was his mother; ever since Della left she called just about every goddam day soon after he came home. He didn't want to answer, but at the fourth ring he reached for the receiver.

"Yes."

"How are you, Leon?"

"Okay."

"Just okay?"

"I'm *okay.*"

"Did you have a hard day?"

"It was okay. The usual."

"I haven't talked to you in a few days."

A few days? Just yesterday!

Wasn't it yesterday?

"It was three days ago," she said. "If I don't call you, I never hear from you. Did you call a lawyer?"

"Mother, I told you I did see a lawyer."

"No, I mean a new lawyer. You said you wanted to see a new lawyer."

"Mother, I can't get to see Freddie yet. They won't let me yet."

"But that's what I told you, Leon. You're the one said you wanted to see a new lawyer."

"I've changed my mind."

"Leon, you shouldn't have hit him the way you did."

"Mother, I hardly touched him!"

"That's not what Della says."

"Mother, we going through this again?"

"I'm—just talking, Leon. When am I going to see you?"

"I—I don't know. I'll call you, I'll be over."

A hesitation. "You sure you're all right?"

Again? "I'm all right!"

"I'm—only asking, Leon."

"But I've told you. I've answered it."

"All right, I'll talk to you. You—you be well, Leon."

He felt like flinging the phone across the room. All the prying! And acting so caring. He couldn't help it, but once in a while when she acted so caring he couldn't help thinking how she'd left him, when he was only ten, left him and his father to live with a guy twenty years younger. And then once she'd married him, she became so goddam fucking moral. "Did you read who Liz Taylor's running around with?" "My neighbor, she's got a son a homosexual."

And then there was that fag business with him.

Not that she'd ever accused him. But he'd been able to tell it in her voice, the way she'd looked at him.

"You really want to be a *nurse*?" And the way she'd kept asking it.

"Yes, I want to. Why do you keep *asking*?"

"Because I'm interested, Leon." But she couldn't fool him. It made him realize she must have always wondered.

This had been when he'd told her he was giving up his job as assistant manager at SuperMarket Henny's, soon after he had started seeing Della.

Della was the one who'd suggested he become a nurse, on their fourth or fifth date. He'd met her at a party one of the fellows at the store took him to. She was five years older, a chubby RN, a college graduate who, from the way she kissed him and squirmed against him when he took her home, probably hadn't had a date in a year.

"No one's home, they're away, don't be nervous." This, when they were on the sofa and he kept looking toward the staircase. But though he was nervous, it wasn't about that. The drumming of his heart went back to when he was about sixteen, and this girl named Annie had gone into the back of his car with him, the first one who'd ever done that. But after he'd had her panties off and reached down for himself, for what he'd thought would be the thick fullness, it had gone down. And when, after trying desperately to will himself hard, he'd finally looked at Annie's face, there was that question in her eyes that maybe he was a queer or something; and though, when he muttered an apology, she said, "It's okay," there was a coolness in her voice and in the way she slipped her panties back on and adjusted her clothes.

Every time after that there was always that icy fear. And he either couldn't get it up or would pop off too quickly.

"Hey, what's the big federal case?"

He'd tried that night with Della, as he almost always tried, but went off as he lowered himself between her legs.

40

"Hey, what's the big federal case?" she kept saying, holding him close. "Hey, come on, hey."

Then she'd said she didn't care if it never happened, that she just wanted to lie here next to him. All she wanted, she said, was to hear all about him, about when he was a boy, about growing up. And it was the same thing on their next three dates—didn't care, just wanted to be close like this, it didn't ever ever have to happen. And that was when, so contrary, the stirring gradually began. "You don't have to," she'd said, which somehow only made it easier for him, and then, though he didn't last long, though he knew he didn't last long, her long hard embrace, her kisses, and her voice against his shoulder saying how wonderful it had been.

"Seriously," she'd said on that fourth or fifth date, "did you ever think of being a registered nurse? Why don't you? Why don't you be a nurse? Stevenson"—a local hospital—"has a great school. I hear they're looking for more men."

He'd had to give it a lot of thought. He'd believed that fag shit himself, and wasn't about to label himself a fag, but once he looked into it, once he saw what it really was, he got a good feeling about it. There was the security—a nurse could always find a job—and he really wanted to help people.

He'd always—maybe until a couple years ago, when things really started going wrong—he'd always wanted to help people. But first his sex went again; he didn't know why. Maybe it was when she started getting fatter. Or when she began treating him like some kind of villain—he couldn't raise his voice to Freddie without her putting her arms around the boy and saying things like everything will be all right. Or maybe it was when he first began suspecting she was seeing someone—nothing he could really put his finger on at the beginning, but things like her "seeing" girlfriends at night she hadn't seen in years. Things like that. But he was afraid to ask, and his sex just kept going. And the harder he tried the worse it was. But she'd never ridiculed him until that one Sunday morning.

He'd awakened about six, hard—the first time in so long. She was lying with her broad back to him, and he put his arm around her, his face against her shoulder. He was afraid to wake her; but with a kind of desperation, afraid it would go away, he began touching her breasts, reaching down through the v of her nightgown. She made little sounds of annoyance, tried to turn away, but then gradually began stirring. Still without opening her eyes, she took his hand and placed it between her legs, began rocking slowly, then faster against it. Then she turned over and waited on her back.

But even as he settled into her, he could feel himself peaking. And though he struggled against it, he was finished in seconds.

She stared at him. "This what you woke me for?"

"Dell, I'm sorry, let me touch—"

"Christ," and she whirled away from him, "why don't you go somewhere and learn how?"

It was two days later that the little girl approached him in the park. He was sitting off by himself reading a paper when she came up to him. She was nine or ten, with a round face and black bangs. Would he like to buy a box of candy for her church? No—but she kept coming back. Finally he set down the paper angrily. She had a saucy little face and large black eyes, which somehow only angered him more. "Go away, go. Don't bother me." He touched her flat little chest with his forefinger, then—all at once wanting to—on the groin. And suddenly he was on his feet in a burst of panic, for the child was running off, screaming.

He started to walk away, stopped, started to run, stopped. It would look wrong if he left, but he couldn't stay . . .

"You!" And there was a policeman striding up the path, with the child and a maid. Then suddenly everything was happening—a siren drawing closer, then the police car and, while people kept streaming in from every section of the park, being shoved handcuffed into the back.

"I didn't do anything! I didn't mean anything!" But the two cops in the front seat didn't even look back at him. "Please, I've got a family, I've never done anything, I didn't do anything to her—please!"

Thank God, though, for the judge at the hearing that evening. "I'm letting you go not only because the parents don't want the child involved anymore, but your record's clean, you've apparently been leading a good life. But if there's ever a next time. . ."

Now tell me the truth, Della had said when they'd come home. "I want the real, real truth. Did you touch her?"

He was sitting on the sofa, crying. "No! Yes! I don't know. Yes."

"Why, for God's sake? A child! A baby."

"I don't know. I didn't mean anything."

"You're crazy, you know that? You know that?"

He raised his head quickly. "Me? *Me?* You bitch! You fucking bitch! If I'm crazy you've driven me crazy!" And then he burst out with it for the first time. "Fucking around! You've been fucking around!"

She stared at him. Then she ran toward him, fists raised, her face so ugly, so full of loathing that he wanted to smash it away. And that was when he'd hit her. Both fists. Bloodied her. Almost killed her. . .

Thinking about it now, he found himself breathing so quickly his chest hurt. He stood up from the bed.

Dawn.

It was suddenly calming to think of her.

There wasn't the self-loathing any more.

Wing—what an interesting name, she'd said the first time.

Feel guilty? she'd said. Why should he feel guilty?

"I just do. I've never done this before."

"Please don't. Please don't. You—I mean this as a compliment, because I think it's a beautiful quality—you must be a very sensitive person."

"I don't know. I guess."

"I think it's a beautiful quality. But please don't feel nervous, please don't feel guilty. There's absolutely nothing to feel guilty or nervous about." He'd be amazed at the kinds of people who called—psychiatrists, psychologists, ministers, celebrities, he'd be amazed at some of the names. "But they're people just like us, people who have problems, needs."

"What kind of problems?"

"Oh, just name it. No one to really talk to. Life's a bore. Husband or wife running around. All kinds of sexual problems, hangups."

"Do any of them say you helped?"

"They say. And it makes me feel good. So, don't be nervous. And certainly not with me. Certainly never, ever with me."

And after all, she said, it's really just a *phone*. Two people talking on a phone. "Okay? So let's start over . . . Hi."

And he could picture a beautiful smile, could feel his tension beginning to ease. . .

What, he finally felt free enough to ask, did she look like?

She'd been a blonde for him then, just as she'd been a blonde for him today. But only a few days ago she'd had long black hair for him, with just a thin chain around her throat. He'd wanted long black hair then, and the chain was something he thought of, during. And she would open when he wanted her to open, and close when he wanted to, and she never criticized and would say whatever he wanted her to. And he could go on so long with her, could hold off; and though sometimes he doubted her, still sometimes it had to be true, sometimes he knew she came with him.

But who was she, really? Where was this phone? In a bedroom, like she said? In her home? Some hotel, maybe, with a wide, clean-sheeted bed?

Today he had pictured her lying on a brocaded lounge, with silk curtains all around.

He made himself stop.

He went downstairs to see what he could make for dinner. But he really wasn't hungry. He settled for some canned soup. Afterward he went to a bar around the corner. He never used to go to bars; in fact, hated drinking. Not that he liked it now. He just wanted to be with—people. No, not people; that wasn't so; he wanted to sit near a woman. He wanted to take a seat next to a woman, and start a conversation, and forget Della and Freddie and that he once touched a little girl, and that something made him keep making these calls.

Wanted to talk to a woman; but the three times he did see a woman alone, and did sit down next to her, he only spoke once. And that was something stupid, like what time is it.

Still, he looked. And once in a while he would wonder: Could this one be Dawn?

# 4

MRS. NORLUND, A slender, handsome woman in her late sixties who lived five houses from Lynn, was driving by as Lynn started to pull into her driveway. She stopped and lowered her window.

"Sweetheart, I hope I didn't embarrass you," she said, her voice lilting with her Norwegian accent.

"No. No, you didn't."

"He said I did . . . Well, I want you to know he was very, very impressed with you."

Lynn smiled. A couple of weeks ago Mrs. Norlund, whom she'd spoken to perhaps four times, had stopped her in the super-market to say she would love to give her name to her stepson, who'd just moved here about a month ago—he was the new news director (or newsman; Lynn couldn't remember which) at Channel 5. Would Lynn mind? No—and that, she thought, would be the end of it. After all, what guy—especially in that field, where they probably had groupies—would call anyone his mother recommended? But then last week, as Lynn was walking toward her house, Mrs. Norlund called to her from up the street and walked over with him. And Mrs. Norlund had been so gushing about her, about Lynn having helped her find a good opthalmologist, that it had been quite awkward for both of them. But he had been very gracious. . . .

"Well, I just wanted to tell you," Mrs. Norlund smiled. "I'll see you. Take care."

"You too. I'll see you."

Lynn had stopped for tires and, while they were being put on, had gone across the street to a small grocery store for a few things—milk, butter, rolls, cupcakes that Rachel liked at bedtime. She shifted the package to her other arm and unlocked the door. As she closed it, she heard, "Hey, my Mom."

Rachel came out of the kitchen, followed closely by her friend Tiffany. Rachel flung her arms around her, kissed her and then, an arm still around her waist, turned to Tiffany. "Hey, what do you think of my Mom? She beautiful?"

Tiffany nodded and smiled. She always seemed to be nodding and smiling when she was with Rachel. If she spoke at all, it was when they were alone.

The girls trailed after her into the kitchen. Remember, Rachel was saying, what she'd told her about Mr. Martin? What she heard? He looked under dresses? Someone who was taking him at summer school just told them too—he was filling a beaker but his eyes were on her legs all the time.

"Oh come on, Rach."

"I'm glad I didn't get Martin. I loved Mr. Goldberg. Could you picture Goldberg looking under dresses?" she asked Tiffany. They both immediately giggled. Then she said, "He's so nice. But *Martin!*"

They started following her up to her bedroom, then broke off when the phone rang in Rachel's room. Tiffany scampered behind her, closing the door. Lynn smiled, looking at the door. Thank God she'd gotten her a phone. She hadn't wanted to, was afraid it would interfere with homework; but it hadn't, she was an excellent student, and it left her own phone open.

She felt good all at once, her mind felt clear. She could hear laughter from Rachel's room, then Tiffany screaming, "Really? Gross!" Loved it. And yet how many young mothers complained—the noise, the strewn clothes; can't wait till they leave, go to college. She couldn't understand it.

She took off her blouse, adjusted the cups of her bra, and

46

slipped into a thin, sleeveless shirt. Jeans now; would have worn them this morning, but she'd thought she might go to still another employment agency during lunch.

More screams, this time from Rachel. And more. Time to be the mother.

"Rach-el." From her doorway.

"Moth-er."

"That's enough. Lower it. Can it."

For some reason this struck the girls as funny. But then again, a lot of strange things struck them as funny. The room gradually grew still. She went back in her room; the zipper on her jeans was broken. She was in her bikini panties looking through her closet for another pair, when Rachel and Tiffany came to the door.

"We're going for pizza, okay?" It was just around the corner.

"No, stay home. I have spinach." She'd climbed into the jeans and was stuffing in her shirt.

"Moth-er."

"Go. I command you to go for pizza. Here's money. Enjoy."

After they left, she looked in the refrigerator to see what she might make for herself. She wasn't particularly hungry or in the mood to go to much trouble. Sipping at a glass of tomato juice, she made an omelet, mixing in scallions and feta cheese, and took it, along with the morning paper, to the small table by the windows. The Pastoris, the young couple to her right, were in their yard, kneeling by the wading pool where their two children were knee-deep and splashing. She looked at them, thinking fleetingly of the time Jon had brought a pool home for Rachel. It was still in the garage, curled and twisted. She opened the paper to the employment section.

She'd already looked through it at lunch, but maybe she'd missed something. No. Copywriter—she couldn't remember when she'd seen the last ad. . . . Sales. Administrative assistant. Secretarial. How many had she been out on?

She checked off a few of the secretarial ads, though she was sure they paid little. If she could even get them.

She became aware suddenly that her heart was racing. She put down the paper, made herself sit back from the table; tried to relax.

She just couldn't go on like this. No way. Had to try to get

47

something, even temporarily. Worry about bills later. And just keep hoping her résumés would pull something in.

In her bedroom she took one of her résumés from a drawer and looked it over. Maybe she should have put down a college degree—wouldn't have to be Harvard, Bryn Mawr; some college in Siberia, a college that went out of existence. And maybe she shouldn't have told the truth about how long she'd been in promotion at Crain & Crain. Instead of just a year, make it three years, five.

She opened her portable and set it on her desk. No, she wouldn't put in college, but she'd add a few years to promotion and hope no one would check that closely. Or write it in a way that would make it seem longer than it was. That had been a mistake. Though it was too late to do anything about the places her résumé had gone out to, she'd already accumulated a list of about twenty-five more.

The front door opened and closed while she was typing. Rachel came up and stood briefly in the doorway. "Would you believe I have to wash my hair again?"

"I never doubted it for a second."

"Tiffany, that pig, she put her greasy hands on my head."

Lynn's phone rang as Rachel walked off. It was an old friend, Nan Voelmer.

"Lynn. I thought you died."

"God, I've been so busy." Such a stupid excuse. But she felt momentarily flustered. "How're you doing? How's Gordon?"

"Fine, fine. How're *you* doing? It's been so long. I told myself, 'Look, you've called twice, if she doesn't want to call you—' But you know me." She had on her kidding voice, but she was serious.

"Tell me," Lynn said brightly, "how've you been?"

"If I said pregnant again?"

"*No.* Oh, great."

They chatted for about fifteen minutes, and by the time they hung up Lynn had promised to meet her for a drink the following week. She went back to her typewriter. But she just sat staring at it. She told herself that the reason she hadn't been in touch with Nan, in fact with all her old friends, was that they were friends

48

she'd made when she was married; that they'd all been couples together.

And it was true, as far as it went.

But wasn't it also, she wondered, that as long as she was doing what she was doing, they could never share worlds?

AT FIRST SHE thought it was morning, that the room was filled with daylight. But then she heard voices and saw with a sinking feeling that she'd fallen asleep with the TV on. Oh Christ. And here she was, wide-awake.

She fumbled around the bed for the remote control, found it, and tried several other channels, looking for a movie, preferably one that was dull, that would help her fall asleep. But everything she clicked on became an irritant. She turned off the set and switched on the lamp next to her bed.

God, only a little after two. She'd gone to bed about twelve.

She went through some magazines in her night-table drawer, pulled out a *Gourmet* and a *Ladies Home Journal.* She riffled through them. But they too were like irritants. She put *Gourmet* aside last.

She'd been subscribing to it for years. She loved cooking, though she wasn't what Jon had called a "natural" cook—that is, though she could follow the most complicated recipe, she generally was afraid to improvise, especially for company. But the wonder was she wanted to cook at all. Since her mother had worked most nights, Lynn often used to have to make dinner for her father and younger brother, and hated it. And the handful of things she'd made she had learned from her mother, who was absolutely the worst cook in the world.

Jon, on the other hand, was a natural. The first time she'd met him, for instance, he'd taken a group of them to his place and between drags on an occasional joint passed along to him, made—substituting ingredients, and with what seemed like a few quick gestures—cioppino. And during the first few years of their marriage, he would cook most of the dinners, though by then she'd really wanted to. It only started to change when he began pulling away from the practice of law, started spending most evenings working on plays; when the first signs of his frustrations began to show. With himself, with her.

It was almost seven months now since the divorce. She'd had a few dates since, but most of the men she'd been out with—the old story—seemed interested only in jumping in bed.

She'd been tempted once or twice, and the thing that dismayed her was that they were, really—not really, but in a way creeps. So it hadn't been for lack of desire.

It was only recently that she really didn't feel any desire.

Sometimes she even wondered—why don't I feel anything?

But those voices—at first they just seemed sick to her. Sick in an abstract way. But they'd become sick of late in a different way. A real sickness, like voices crying out from wards. Give me this, give me that. Be this, be that. Let me see your white ass, let me feel those big tits, suck me, hold me, are you doing it too, are you really doing it? I'm a lawyer, I'm a flier, I've never done this before, my wife wants nothing to do with me, what's your real name, can I meet you, can I see you. . .

The voices.

The voices, it seemed, of just about every man in the world.

# 5

SITTING IN HIS car, double-parked, Leon stared at the little brick house diagonally across the street. Della's parents' house—she'd moved in with them. It was a few minutes after midnight, and the place was dark.

Her car was out there, all right—it was the first thing he'd looked for. The second, actually—the first was the chink's car. But he couldn't make it out in the line of cars parked solid along the curb. Which could mean they were out together, or he just didn't remember the chink's car.

He pictured them in there, on the sofa, Freddie, her parents, asleep upstairs.

She'd fuck him with Freddie upstairs, she'd do that.

He looked again at the cars. It was a Chrysler, wasn't it? He was sure he'd seen them drive off that day in a Chrysler.

He had pleaded with himself not to check on her, had tried to convince himself he was just imagining; but for four days in a row he had left his shift early and driven from his hospital to her hospital's lot, in time to see the seven-to-three shift come off. Three days she got into her car and drove straight home. The fourth, she walked over to another car and got in on the passenger side. Then the chink walked over and slid in—and they were off and gone, while he tried to get past a car that cut in front of him.

"How'd it go today?" He had tried to act so casual when she came home.

"Okay. Same as usual." And she'd set down a bag of groceries she'd picked up on the way.

And he'd never said anything, though it kept killing him, not only her fucking, not only *that*, but—he'd read this somewhere— that chinks could hold off for ever—that it was in their religion or blood where it was like a sin not to make a woman come.

It killed him, thinking of her coming and coming. And yet he'd never said anything until it burst out of him that night of the hearing, because even though she was a fucking whore, he was, God help him, scared to lose her, scared to go back to nothing.

So many times he'd wanted to kill her.

Like now, wishing he had a machine gun, a hatchet, anything.

He fought to calm down.

Why'd he even drive up here? He wasn't going to get any pictures at *night*. Why did he drive twenty miles to sit double-parked and stare at the house? He'd even asked himself this all the way up here.

He could see himself doing this a couple of times, but ten-twelve times in the six weeks since she'd left? And even if he got a picture of the chink going in or out, what did that mean, a guy going in and out of her parents' house? And all he ever got, anyway, was a shot one afternoon of her taking out the trash. And he'd even *developed* it.

... What was that, a police car? He couldn't tell, just that the car driving slowly through the intersection down the block seemed to have something on its roof. He wasn't doing anything, it wasn't against the law, he would imagine, but he didn't want to be found here. He drove off slowly, but felt an aching loneliness as he started to leave the street, and he made a fast U-turn and circled the block and passed the house again. Inched past the house, looking it over. Then he sped off toward home.

A few miles away he stopped at a taproom, walked in, and stood by the door, looking around. There were only a few people at the large circular bar watching an overhanging TV. . . . Was that a woman sitting alone? No, a goddam young punk with long hair. The only woman there was sitting with a man in a plaid shirt; they looked alike, and were even laughing alike at something the bartender said. He went back to his car. Several miles down the road he stopped at another place. This was a lot more crowded. There were several women, but only one he could see who seemed to be alone.

He walked over. He wished he could sit right next to her, but there were two empty seats and he felt he had to take the farthest one. He ordered a beer and sipped at it slowly.

He saw, from the edges of his eyes, that she wasn't bad looking. About thirty-five or so. She was looking toward the far ceiling, smiling slightly to herself.

He wondered how to start. There was always the time, what time is it? Or, do you come here often? But if it ever came to what do you do, *and what do you do,* the one thing he'd never say was a nurse. Oh, they didn't say it but you could see the fag thing in their look.

"Do you come here often?"

It just came out of him. And how dumb, how stupid.

She leaned toward him a little. "Pardon, I didn't hear you."

"I said I was noticing they serve nice size drinks. I've never been here before."

"Oh." She nodded, with that same smile, then looked away again.

He sat looking ahead, feeling a vague touch of disappointment that it wasn't Dawn's voice.

He made believe he was looking away, but actually he kept glancing at her. Then he saw her lift herself a little from the stool, and she was smiling at a man coming in the front door. He came over and took the stool next to her.

Leon finished his drink slowly and drove toward home again. He dreaded going there, wondered why the hell he'd just renewed the lease—they'd only been renting it. Oh, he knew— but should have known better. Kids were as ungrateful as women. He'd kept the house instead of moving into an apartment be- cause he thought maybe Freddie would change his mind and say he'd rather live with him. And then there were all the things he'd bought for him, especially in the past year or so when the marriage started slipping fast: a motorbike, a twelve-speed regular bike, a billiard table so big they almost couldn't get it in the basement, a ham radio, a twenty-two rifle, a little battery-powered car he could get in and *drive,* for Christ sake; he couldn't remember all the things. And there was Della yelling, "You're crazy, he's too young for half these things, he's only ten, he's gonna kill himself, kill someone, and we can't afford them anyway!" But he wanted Freddie to have them. And then what happens? "I want to live with my Mommy! My *Mommy!*"

No wonder he'd hit him that one time he saw him, out on the sidewalk. But it was nowhere as bad as they said. Just a slap. Still, it should have been her. She poisoned his mind against him, that bitch.

Another taproom, this one about six miles from home. He pulled into the parking lot. From the number of cars, obviously crowded. He turned off the motor but didn't take the key from the ignition. He'd been here twice before, months ago; each time had a couple beers, watched them play shuffleboard, darts; watched them talking in cliques or shouting at a game on TV. Always the outsider. The one time he felt he could pick up a woman, he'd chickened out.

Should he go in?

What was the point?

He found himself staring at the entrance to the taproom. A woman in a strapless cotton dress had stepped out, was holding onto a post near the door. She seemed to have come out for air, or to get sick; he was sure someone would come after her. But she let go of the post and began walking his way. Stiffly. He could see in the light of a street lamp a little fixed smile on her lips.

He watched her. Then, his heart galloping, he slid out.

"Can I help you, Miss?"

She stopped, looked at him, frowning. Then the same smile came back.

"My, aren't you sweet," she said.

SHE WAS SITTING naked on the edge of the bed, staring up at him, a skinny woman in her late forties, with strawlike hair, and a mottled flush of excitement between her thin breasts.

"You have gone and made me chilly," she said, smiling, her arms crisscrossed over her breasts, fingers on her shoulders, thighs pressed together.

Leon, fully dressed, stared at her. Go home. Leave. Nothing was going to happen, could happen, with her.

Why did he let it get to this? All the way to her home she'd talked, rambling on. About the heat, and how she wished she could live at the seashore, any seashore. Then about going to her high school reunion a few weeks ago, and how depressing it was, everyone so old. And about her husband, dead some twelve years, and she thought of him every day, but she had a nice life, she had this nice job at Blaedon's—you know, the specialty shop?—she sold handbags, everyone there was so nice. And then, at her door, would he like a drink—a real drink, or a drink of water? And though he told himself to leave, he said yes, a drink of water, and they stood by her refrigerator while he drank the water he didn't want, feeling sorry for her, somehow remembering that student nurse in his class who confided in him, crying, that she'd been with five interns and she didn't know why, didn't know why. You just push a button, he didn't want to push the button, yet he did. Just a kiss, and her arms were around him, all over him. And now this.

Leave!

But—maybe. He began unbuttoning his shirt, his fingers thick on each button. He felt hollow deep in his stomach. His heart had the fear-beat he'd known all his life.

"Leon," she said. "That's such a pretty name. Did I tell you you remind me of my husband? He didn't have your color hair, and he was shorter—a little heavier—but there is something."

She squeezed her shoulders tighter. Her eyes, with that little smile below, remained fixed on his face as he bent down to take off his shoes and step out of his pants. He sat next to her and put his arms around her. Her arms closed around him. She smelled terribly of booze, though she'd sobered up considerably. She kissed him with her teeth clamped closed, but she mashed herself against him so tightly that she was kissing him with the insides of her lips. Then she opened her mouth, and bit him very lightly on the tongue, and drew it in.

She slid out of his arms to lay back. She watched him sitting there. Then, with that same smile, she held out her arms. He lay next to her, kissing her about the face, his eyes closed, hands pressing her breasts, then the bones that seemed to be trying to protrude from her little plaster white buttocks.

He grabbed her wrist as she suddenly reached for him. He didn't want her to feel—nothing. She mustn't feel nothing! He arched his body away from her slightly, still kissing her furiously. He was suddenly aware she was lying still.

"Make love to me," she said.

The fear-beat was growing. He looked at her. "Tell me what you want me to do to you."

"Just make love to me."

He lay back, looking at the ceiling. What was the use?

She said quietly, "You're a good-looking man, Leon. I've never attracted such a good-looking man."

He was aware, slowly, that her hand was working him. He started to reach for her wrist, then his hand fell away and he closed his eyes. Nothing, but it didn't matter any more. She was no one he had to please, no one he'd see again. And it wasn't his fault, it was hers. There was a vaguely sour smell about her; there were all those thin veins on her breasts, on her legs.

. . . Blonde or black? Blonde at first, long and blonde; but no, black, long and black, framing her oval face and waterfalling over her white shoulders. She kissed him softly on the lips, moist and soft. Top? Did he want her on top? Bottom? Top, so he could see those plump breasts, reach up for them, cup them, feel the texture, the nipples, suck. No, bottom. This time bottom, so he could see her face in exquisite anguish.

But as he lifted himself above her, the hair was becoming strawlike again, and the lips the insides of lips, and the veins were back, and the smells . . . He felt himself soften, tried frantically to press it in with his fingers, couldn't, and at the same time, so perversely, began releasing.

Sitting up, he began pawing around the bed for his shorts. He

56

didn't want to meet her eyes, just wanted to run. He could see her hand rubbing the sheet against her thighs. "I'm sorry."

"There's nothing to be sorry about. We've got all night."

He pulled on his shorts, stood up. He'd still barely looked at her.

"Where you going?"

"I—I've got to go."

"Where"—her voice had suddenly become coy; she was on her knees on the bed, trying to look into his face—"where you going?"

He looked at her.

Get away! He felt sick.

"Leon."

Get away.

"Lee-on." She was tugging at his arm. "Where you going?"

He whirled back.

Smash her! Smash that ugly face. Smash her! Rip her face, her eyes, grab something—go grab it, that lamp, that lamp, pound her, obliterate that face, smash those teeth, those breasts, smash them—

He felt himself slowly go limp.

She seemed to be forming through a fog, taking shape, still on her knees, her face sad and troubled now.

"What did I do wrong, Leon?"

He yanked on his pants, fighting his foot through a twisted trouser leg, fumbling with the zipper.

"Leon, what did I do wrong?"

Why couldn't he get his shirt on?

"Leon?"

Buttoning it frantically, he hurried to the stairs. He almost ran to his car.

IN HIS HOUSE, he slumped down on the sofa. He was trembling.

Dear God—almost.

First—a little girl. To touch her. And now this, almost killed—A few more seconds—

He sat there, trying to concentrate on his breathing. And as he did, he became more aware of the house, the darkness, the silence, that except for Harry he was all alone. . . .

If he could only meet her.

"Why," she'd said gently, "are you upset about that?"

It had been on his very first call, when it had happened to him in seconds, as though she were right there with him, and he'd mumbled something about being sorry. "Why are you upset about that?" she said. "Don't you know that's flattering to a woman?" And when it happened again, on the second call, "Why are you apologizing? Why?" Wing, you're too hard on yourself, she said. Wing, you're a very sensual person, she said. Just relax, don't worry about it, just relax. . .

And soon after that it became it's too much, Wing, you're too much.

He wouldn't fail with her. Not her.

It was maddening—knowing there was one person beyond reach who could make you whole.

# 6

---

MISS STOCKER ROSE from her desk and extended her hand as Lynn entered her cubicle, one of many into which the T. L. Rain employment agency was divided. An attractive, scrubbed-looking young woman whose smile even looked efficient, she said, "It's nice seeing you again."

"It's nice seeing you." Lynn had called her almost exactly at nine this morning, then had to call Master's to say she'd be late.

"So, let's see," Miss Stocker said. She'd already pulled Lynn's résumé from her files, and had it on top of a neat pile on her desk. She began going over it, pursing her lips as she turned to the second page, then came back to the first. "I only wish," she said, still reading, "I had something in your field. But like I said, there hasn't been an opening in months."

I see, she said, looking at a paper attached to it, that you've already taken the typing test.

"Yes." That had really galled her. This was one of the first agencies she'd been to; and, like a couple of others she went to, they'd had her take a typing test even though she'd been looking for a copywriting job. Because, no doubt, she was female. . .

Looking up, Miss Stocker said, "I only wish you had a medical or

59

legal background. I've got a few great spots open there as an executive secretary, but you'd need experience." She began looking through a loose-leaf book, pausing now and then to look at a page, then turning it.

Lynn said, "As I said, I'll take just about anything."

She'd been so sure, when she called, that she'd have no trouble getting a secretarial job once she told them she wasn't looking for any particular salary; but anxiety was building as Miss Stocker slowly kept turning pages. Miss Stocker reached for another book, then set it down.

She sat for a moment, her left hand in her hair. "Look," she said finally, "let me tell you quite frankly what the problem is. I really can't justify sending you out on any of these jobs—I know you won't stay."

"That's not fair. How can you say that?"

"For one thing, your salary history's too high for any of these jobs. And on top of that, you're really looking for something else. You're not going to stay. I can't do it. Let's wait till I have something better—"

"Please, I need something."

"Mrs. Shephard, I can't recommend you for a little secretarial job, a little typing job, when you were last making—what?" She looked again. "Twenty-three-five. I can't do it. And even if I did, they'd see this salary, they'd think something's wrong with us here."

"Would they have to know?"

"If you come through this office, yes."

Lynn said, "What about something temporary? You run a temporary service, don't you?"

"Yes. I'll put you down for that. But really—Look, I hate to be discouraging, but we've got an awful lot of people. So I don't know when you'll get a call. I just want you to know that. But I will put you down."

Lynn stood up. Miss Stocker stood up with her, then said, "Look, I hope you don't think this was a waste of time. It wasn't. It gave me an opportunity to refresh my mind about you, and I'm going to be trying. Something's bound to break."

"Fine."

Lynn walked out through the maze of cubicles to the waiting room, where seven or eight people were sitting on school-type chairs with arms to write on, most of them filling out applications. She walked out to the elevators, as though from a dark movie house into glare: into a world by the bank of elevators where suddenly everyone seemed to have jobs, were carrying attaché cases or were chatting on their way back to their offices or standing making plans for lunch.

A world that all at once seemed enclosed in glass, impossible to reenter.

SHE GLANCED AT the dashboard clock as she drove. Almost two hours late. The Hadleys must be having a fit.

"I'll be in in about an hour or two," she'd told Tina. But she hadn't worried about it then—after all, she'd soon be getting another job.

She started to pull past the car in front, but had to drift back because of oncoming traffic. She tried twice more before making herself settle down.

Calm it, cool it.

She was angry at herself.

Scared to lose *that* job? Still didn't know her own worth?

It was like she was that kid again in the peeling, green frame house with the horrible red trim, gathering up nerve to tell her mother she'd like to try college; wondering did she have brains enough or even the right to try, when her girlfriends were going on to places like cosmetology school or hoping to get a job in a department store or insurance company.

"College?" Her mother had looked at her with a slight tilt of her head—they'd never even *talked* about it before. "That's—nice, but isn't it a lot of money?"

"No, I'll probably go to community college. It won't be much. And I'll be working."

"You know what you want to be? You never said."

"I don't know. I just want to go to school."

Her mother looked at her and then, with that bright, red-lipsticked smile of hers, said, "Hey," and hugged and patted her.

Like that kid again, who gave up college to help make her

61

husband a lawyer; who gave him every support while he tried to write plays, and yet, when she showed him the first thing she wrote for Crain & Crain—

He read it at his desk while she stood nervously in the hallway—three pages she'd worked on every evening for more than a week. Then he held them out to her. "It's okay." And he turned back to his typewriter.

Her heart plummeted. She was about to ask if he had any suggestions, but his face was fixed darkly on his work—a look, she was sure, he hadn't had just before. She walked downstairs. Soon he began yelling where was his ballpoint pen, why couldn't he keep anything around here?

She never, of course, showed him anything else she wrote.

Well, she might be worried now, scared, she might have to keep going neck-deep through shit to get where she wanted, but she'd never go back to any of that.

TEN MINUTES AFTER the camp bus left her off, Rachel was in the shower, shampooing her hair. Stepping out onto the mat, she toweled herself hard, then looked closely at her face in the long mirror on the door. The zit on her chin was almost gone. She tried to resist looking at what Tiffany, with her big boobs, called the mosquito bites under her nipples, but she did give them a fast look, telling herself she wasn't really checking; more important, didn't really care. In her room, with its array of stuffed animals and a huge poster of a rainbow over the headboard of her bed, she sat cross-legged on the floor and ran the blower.

The ringing of the phone cut through the loud, hot whirring. It was, as she knew, Tiffany, though they'd been with each other all day. One or the other always called soon after she came home. Tiffany wanted to know did she really think Liz liked Michael, and when Rachel said that's what Tracy told her, Tiffany said she didn't think much of Liz then, if she liked *him.* Jason, though, was cute, didn't she think?

*"Cute?"*

"Don't you think he's cute?"

"Oh no."

"I think he's . . . sorta cute. Look," she said hurriedly, "gotta go. Gotta go to the store."

"Call me."

"Call me."

"Call me."

Rachel finished drying her hair, then looked at the clock. Her mother should be home soon. She felt so bad her mother had to work this hard. And sometimes it scared her that she seemed tired lately and, though she still smiled a lot and they had fun, worried . . .

She was trying to decide what to wear, when her mother peered into her room.

"How's my Mom?" She lifted her face for a kiss.

"Good. How are you, sweetheart?"

"Okay."

"Tell me about your day."

Rachel followed her into her room. "Oh, the same. You know."

"No, I don't. Did you have horseback riding?"

"No, tomorrow."

"What did you have for lunch?"

"Macaroni and cheese. Gu-ross."

"Did you at least get a lot of it?"

"Oh ho."

"What do you say you get dressed? We'll go some place nice to eat."

Rachel went into her room, picked out a fresh polo shirt. She called, "How nice?"

"What do you mean how nice?" Lynn called back.

"Can I wear shorts?"

"We're not going to the Ritz, dear. Yes."

Rachel put on a pair of blue shorts. She loved being with her. Tiffany, most of the other kids, couldn't believe she was so tight with her. They'd sometimes talk in the most awful ways about their Moms.

As for him, though, she hated him, she really did. Didn't care— really meant this—didn't care if she ever saw him again. Why should she when he didn't want to see her?

Off somewhere with some little pig!

She sat down on her bed, her chest suddenly heaving.

Try not to hate him, her Mom said. Not hate him!

She waited until she calmed down, then slipped on a moccasin. "Mom?"

"Yes," Lynn called from her room.

"Did most people know the colors?"

"What colors, sweetheart?"

*What* colors! Yesterday, when she'd asked her Mom what she'd be working on today, she said she'd be trying to find out how many people knew the new colors on some cereal box.

"Mo-ther! Are you going see-nile?" It was the second time something like this had happened this week.

Silence.

Her mother was walking into the room now, brushing at something on her skirt. "You mean on the new package?"

But why was her face so red?


LYNN HAD TO reach for the phone almost the moment she hung up. Tina, at the console, said, "It's Wing."

She reached down with one hand and scratched her ankle. "Hi."

Nothing.

"Hi," she said. "This is Dawn."

Still nothing. Most of the girls had clients who called them regularly, and he was one of hers. But the only thing that stood out about him was the name, and that he was one of those who paid in advance.

"Hello," she said.

Faintly, "Hello."

"Wing?" He sounded drunk. "This is Dawn."

"You—love me?"

It jolted her. It didn't come across as something light.

"Say you love me."

The words wouldn't come out. Somehow it would be worse than an obscenity.

"Say you love me! Say you love me!"

She held the receiver away from her ear. When she brought it back, there was silence.

64

She said, "Hello?"

But he'd hung up. Slowly, she put the receiver back on the hook.

She was trembling; her flesh had gone cold.

Why should that, of all things, terrify her?

# 7

THE INSTANT SHE hung up, Lynn buzzed the switchboard. "Tina, would you hold the calls? I need a minute."

"Sure, dear."

But Tina wasn't satisfied with that; she knocked on the door, then looked in briefly. "Are you all right? You sound terrible."

"Just a little headache," she lied. "I'll be fine."

"Want to wait till after lunch? It's only a couple minutes."

"Thanks."

"Need some aspirin?"

"No, I have some."

She waited until Tina left, then closed her eyes. She was aware of a quick beating running through her. Why should that have jolted her like this? The first week here, the first calls, the first call in particular, of course, had been terrifying. It had been almost as if the office walls were made of clear plastic, that the men behind the voices were watching her; that they could materialize through the plastic or would be waiting outside on the street. But it had eased away, as Manya had assured her it would.

There was a little knock on the door again, then Manya's voice. "Lunch?"

"Yes, coming."

She went into the washroom first; a few handfuls of cold water on her face helped. Louise and a pretty thing named Peggy, who looked like she should be riding in horse shows, remained at the phones; Mary Hadley, who nearly always wore a hat in the office, had come up from her husband's office to man one of the others.

They went to a luncheonette a couple of blocks away. After they'd ordered sandwiches and iced tea, Manya took a picture from her wallet. "My granddaughter."

"Oh, she's beautiful."

"Did you ever see my daughter, my son-in-law?"

"I don't think so, no."

She handed over a small picture of a bride and groom, cheeks together, smiling.

"They're a handsome couple."

"He," as Manya had already told her several times, "is an electrical engineer. She's going to go back to teaching as soon as the baby's a little older."

Lynn kept looking at it. From what Manya had told her, he was the only one who'd raised any objections to what she was doing; her daughter, after some initial shock that "I knew all the words she did," seemed to get a kick out of it. Lynn handed it back. She felt a little awkward not showing her Rachel's picture in return — after all, Manya not only knew about Rachel but, when Lynn was in a quandary about where to say she worked, Manya was the one who advised saying Master Surveys — after all, Rachel would never learn a thing even if she called Lynn there. But she still didn't want to show her picture.

After the sandwiches and the drinks came, Manya said, "Oh, we got good news yesterday. You know that double-lot I told you Sam bought? He's made quite a profit. Everyone said, don't buy, don't buy, it's higher than it'll ever get. Well. My Sam knew more than all of them. He's a real genius when it comes to real estate. Whatever he touches. I told you he had a heart attack four years ago, didn't I?"

"Yes." Several times.

"We thought it was the end of the world. He had this beautiful clothing store—men's clothing—but the malls were knocking the hell out of him, the doctor said you go back to it, you go back to all that strain, I don't guarantee anything. We thought it was the end of the world. I take this job, and Sam turns out to be a real estate genius. He'd like me to quit. Not that he has anything against it, but he's one of those old-fashioned men who thinks the wife should be at home. But I like doing this, I really do. I got a big mouth. I got a good imagination. And I've always liked helping people. When I was this high, I was the one always bringing home the sick cats. I was always the one kids came to with their problems. Even my mother used to come to me, a kid. I should have been a psychologist. So why should I quit?"

Lynn looked at her. "I got a very weird call just before."

"So what else is new?"

"No, I'm serious. It scared me."

"I'm sorry, I'm always joking, sometimes I forget."

Lynn told her about the call. Manya said, puzzled. "That never happened to you before?"

"Not that way. 'Say you love me.' Just about screaming it. Then hanging up."

"You said weird, I thought of the call I just got. Make believe teacher's going to flunk him, so he stays after school and she, uh, gives him an A. *That's* weird."

"But this was very frightening."

"What did you say?"

"I don't think I said anything. I was just stunned."

"And he just hung up?"

"Yes."

"What do you know about him?"

"Nothing. He never says anything about himself."

"You know what it reminds me of? A kid calling a stranger and yelling a dirty word into the phone and then hanging up. It's like that was his dirty word. Did he ever do anything like that before?"

"No. He's been after me to meet him, but, you know, that's not exactly new . . . What if it happens again? What do you suggest I say?"

"Well, this is a guy who's obviously not getting love too many places. Wife, girlfriend. May have just been fired. Kids got married and left home. Big, empty blank. Me, if it was me I'd just—switch the tone a little. 'Doll, you know I love you.' Doll him to death. Keep throwing it back to him in that tone. Or turn him over to someone else. Me. When I get through with him he won't know which of us to take to the prom."

Lynn smiled. Manya seemed to enjoy having made her smile, then she reached for the menu.

"Let's," Manya said, "think dessert."

LYNN FOLLOWED LOUISE'S waddling rear down the staircase. Like the legendary fat person with dainty feet, she had a thin, coy voice, with a touch of breathlessness to it—a breathlessness, Lynn felt, that must be linked to high blood pressure. In a way, she reminded Lynn a little of herself—she did things quickly, her thoughts always seemed to be racing ahead. And she'd been divorced years ago, and had raised a son, who—she'd just announced as they headed downstairs—had called yesterday to say he had lost his job and he and his wife were moving in with her.

"I swear, you think they're out of the house, they're back again. I hate to talk about Donnie, I love him, but I told him, 'Donnie, don't quit college, you can always get married,' but he quits college and marries this air head—I swear, that's what she is, and she has only four bottom teeth—he marries her, and one week he's a mechanic, the next week he's house painting. I'm going to be working until I'm ninety."

Manya had preceded them outside. Sam, the cigar jutting from his molelike face, was slowly following her around the car to open her door.

"Good night," Manya called.

"Night."

"Night."

Louise sounded out of breath as they walked. Lynn didn't know, or care, if that story about her once working in a whore house was true; all she knew was that this was one hard-working lady, and she liked her for it. She'd been in a number of businesses, all of which had apparently failed—a messenger service, a print shop, had invested in some kind of invention that never took off, worked off and on as a secretary—and had recently confided in

70

Lynn that she was planning on starting her own "telephone shop."

As they neared Lynn's car, she said, "Did he ever say hello to you?"

"Her husband? No."

"You know the only words I ever heard him say? I was walking by them and I heard him say, 'Should we buy the fish?'"

"What's that?" Lynn laughed.

Louise was laughing too. "Honest to God, should we buy the fish? I never heard him say anything before or after that."

"That's funny."

"Should we buy the fish. But he seems nice. And she's a doll, I love her. And she's got a beautiful family, I've been over there several times."

"And he didn't talk then?"

"Not really. but he adores her. See how he follows her around? But I guess he should. What I hear, she's always been the bread-winner. But it's nice, she builds him up to people like he's Einstein."

Lynn was tempted to ask about the real estate deals, but didn't. She really didn't care to know. Let Manya have her fantasies too.

AS SHE PULLED into her driveway, her neighbor, George Pastori, waved to her from his open porch. When she got out of the car he came over to the hedge, his three-year-old son, his youngest, on his shoulders. He said, "How's it going?"

"Good . . . Robbie, you're so *tall,* I can't reach you." She held up her hand to his cheek; grinning, he pulled back.

"I'm on my Daddy."

"You're on your *Daddy.* I thought you'd grown." She said to George, "How's Sara? Tommy? I haven't talked to her for a while."

"Fine, everyone's fine." Look, he wanted her to know they were leaving on vacation at the end of the week, were taking the van up to Canada. "We'll be away three weeks. I know Sara'll be talking to you, but I'd appreciate your keeping an eye on the house."

"Of course."

He began bouncing Robbie on his shoulders. Laughing, Robbie held on to his father's hair.

In the house, she found a note on the dining room table from Rachel that she was at Tiffany's and would be home soon. As she started upstairs, her thoughts drifted back to the Pastoris. The four of them were like something out of Norman Rockwell. And they did so many beautiful things as a family . . .

Envy, girl?

A little. Why not?

Or maybe not envy. Just—thinking.

Of what was undoubtedly the happiest day in her life, Jon in a scrub suit holding her hand and Dr. Jensen saying, "Push harder, push harder, yes, yes," and then, "It's a girl, you've got a beautiful girl," and Jon kissing her, and then her wanting to see the fingers and toes, suddenly petrified because the bottom of one foot was black, too scared to call it to their attention until she realized that they must have footprinted her beautiful little baby.

Of that day, and then of a hot afternoon at Fort Lauderdale— she and a girlfriend from college had come down that morning— and seeing these two handsome guys on the blanket near theirs, the one closest to her with the most interesting face. "We," she whispered to Katy, "have dates tonight."

"Yeah."

She fixed her eyes on a point about three inches from the tip of his nose so she could never be accused of staring at him; fixed it there until he turned, then she glanced away as he smiled. He was still smiling when she looked back. And then he began it: what's your name, what's yours, where you from, where you staying? Then Jon and his friend brought their blanket closer.

Later, after most of the people were gone and the seagulls came flocking in, she and Katy went back to change, then went over to the boys' place, where several other kids had crowded in and Jon made the cioppino and she'd let them talk her into puffing on a joint—the second, and last, she'd ever had. He'd tried to kiss her that night, but she didn't want it—maybe because she was so burned and chilled by the sun; and she was sure that was the last she'd be seeing of Jon Shephard. But he had showed up the next day, concerned about her burn; but she felt better and, fortunately for her, the sky was dark with clouds so that she wouldn't have to go on the beach. He asked had any of them ever been to Key West, and none of them had; so he and his friend rented a car and the four of them drove out to the Keys.

It had still been cloudy when they reached Key West, and it was only there, when they were going through Hemingway's old house, that she found out he wanted to be a writer as well as a lawyer. She even remembered when he said it; he'd been petting one of the million cats there, one of those six-toed descendants of Hemingway's cats when, without looking up at her, he said he wanted to write plays, that he could never be satisfied only with law. It was such an exciting thing to hear—the place, even his looks: with his long hair, he even seemed to *look* like a playwright. And then later, wouldn't you know, the clouds even opened up and, standing out on the dock, arms around each other, they were bathed in one of those miracle Key West sunsets.

From that to the ugliness years later?

She still didn't know when their marriage started to go. She placed it about two years ago, though it probably was before that. But two years ago was when the frustration over his writing began to show, when his remarks weren't just biting but out-and-out vicious.

Like that time he'd asked her what she thought of a play they'd watched on TV. She said, "I thought it was entertaining," because it was, and she hadn't realized he would take that simple comment as an attack on a play he'd written that was also about an old doctor. "You're stupid, you know that? You're so goddam stupid. But what do you expect? You've never even read a decent book."

How many times she'd heard she was stupid, had gotten married only to have a kid, was just like her mother, a lamebrain, all she had to do was dye her hair bright red and she'd be her mother.

And, like the lamebrain she really was, she bought part of it, for much of her was still caught up in that street kid, the kid with a Jew for a father who, though she loved him deeply, probably denied him a hundred times by trying to be the leader at everything but school. So, she'd been the first of her girlfriends to smoke a full cigarette—what was she, ten?—and could say fuck you with the best of them. And knew how to be provocative—like that time with Joey McGinley, when she was maybe fourteen. They were taking a shortcut across a vacant lot one evening when he showed her a long piece of bark with a hole in it.

He touched the hole. "You know what this is?"

Instead of not answering or saying something to make him feel stupid, she said, "It's a hole."

"You ever see a nicer hole than this?"

"I've seen better holes."

"Better holes than this?"

"Oh, yeah. That hole's nothing."

But when he suddenly kissed her, his hand grabbing her wrist and trying to get her to touch him, she knee-ed him and ran.

He'd apparently been as surprised about her as Jon was years later.

She'd come to Bethesda, where he had an apartment while going to school in Washington, and stayed with him for the first time. As she lay in bed with him, feeling more stupid than nervous as they tried, he suddenly stopped and looked at her in astonishment. A virgin?

LEON SAID, "DELLA, it's me, please don't hang up."

There was silence.

"Della?"

Quietly at first, then her voice rising, "What do you want? Why are you calling? I told you never call!"

"Della, please."

"Whatever you have to say, call my lawyer. Have your lawyer call my lawyer, I don't—"

"Della—" His voice broke. "Please—Please, let me see Freddie. Just once. I want to see Freddie. Please."

"Freddie! How many times we got to go through this?"

"Please?" He was crying. "Just for ten minutes? Five minutes?"

She said nothing for a moment. Then, her voice quiet again, "You know his psychiatrist says not yet, it's best not yet. He's still mixed up, depressed. Still doesn't want to. So if you love him— God, if you like him—you'll let him alone, give him time."

"Just—five minutes. *Ask* Freddie. Just ask him. You can be there when we—"

"I don't want to be there."

"Or your mother. Anyone. I just want to see him."

There was a long silence. She said, "I'll talk to him. If he wants to, we'll see."

"Just ask him. Please." He wiped at his eyes. "Just ask him."

"I said I would. That's enough, I said I would."

Lowering the phone, he sat with his head in his hands. She wouldn't ask, he was sure she wouldn't.

It had grown dark outside all at once. He made no move to turn on a light.

Had no one, absolutely no one.

Not even Dawn any more. He'd had one drink—no, two. Just two drinks and those words had poured out. And then to just hang up!

How could he ever call back?

He stood up, wondering where to go, what to do. A bar? . . . But he didn't want to leave here, wanted to be here in case the phone rang.

He put on some lights, then found himself being drawn upstairs; felt the need to go to Freddie's room and just look in. But he stopped himself and sat down on the sofa, knowing from a hundred times before how much harder it was to look into the room at night, everything so bare, even the sheet and pillow gone. Most of the stuff Della hadn't wanted Freddie to take was in the garage—the twenty-two, the motorbike, the Swiss Army knife.

"Get rid of them!" she'd screamed when she saw the guns—the twenty-two Winchester for Freddie, the twenty-two Colt hand-gun for himself. "I don't want them in the house! He's gonna kill himself, you're going to drive him crazy all the shit you buy! He's going to need a psychiatrist."

The guns, he'd bought the guns so they could go to target practice, father and son. She didn't know, lived in some dream world, that this wasn't a safe world any more; he loved helping people, he'd sit at a bedside for hours, turn himself inside out, but this wasn't a safe world, there were people out there who would hurt you . . . And even Freddie had cried he wanted the gun, he wanted the gun.

Freddie! . . . "I want to be with my *Mommy*! My Mommy!"

Forgot it all, everything—the bikes, the gun, everything.

And here he was sitting like a jackass, waiting for a call.

What he ought to do for the first time in his life was something for himself. He had twelve thousand in the bank, and he ought to go out and buy a new car—his was a real junker, everything for *them*; buy a new car and quit his job and take off. Go to California maybe, or Arizona or—

He stood up quickly. The phone was ringing.

"All right," Della said. "All right, just this once. But God help you . . . God help you, if you aggravate that boy!"

FREDDIE'S HAIR, HE thought, was too long. But she always liked it long.

Leon struggled not to say anything about it; he mustn't ruin anything. He said, "So you like being catcher."

"Yeah. It's good."

They were sitting on a bench in a playground near his grandparents' house. Nearby, a couple of mothers were pushing their children on swings.

Leon said, "You used to like outfield." Yet what he wanted to say, but again held himself back, was that you're too little, too skinny, to be catcher. He could get hurt . . .

"Yeah, I like outfield. But you do more, catching."

"That's great." He wasn't as edgy as at the beginning, but he had to be on guard not to say anything wrong that would get back to Della. Freddie, though, seemed to have become relaxed.

"And you do a lot of swimming."

"Yeah, we go to Grandmom and Grandpop's swim club a lot."

"That's nice. Hey, that reminds me. Remember that time we rented that house on the bay?"

Yeah, Freddie laughed, where they caught all those crabs and one got out of the pot. "And you picked it up with a broom and a stick."

"A broom and a dustpan."

"Why'd you put it back in the bay?"

"Oh, you know. I felt the little bugger escaped, he was entitled. That was a real nice place," Leon said.

"Yeah."

76

Leon looked at him. He dreaded looking at his watch. He had promised a half hour; it had to be that. Almost over, yet most of the time they'd just walked, awkward, talking about things like what movies Freddie had seen.

"Freddie?"

Freddie raised his face to him.

"I—I just want you to know I'm sorry. About that time. I didn't mean to hit you. I mean, I shouldn't have."

Freddie looked uncomfortable again. "That's okay."

"It's not okay. I'm sorry. I really hurt you." His eyes started to fill. "I could have broken something."

"That's okay."

Leon reached out and touched the boy's cheek. "I want you to know something. I love you. You know that?"

Freddie shrugged. Then he nodded.

Leon said, "I do. I want you to know that," and then wondered if that was one of the wrong things to say. It wouldn't only go back to Della, but to the damn psychiatrist.

There wasn't a psychiatrist alive he trusted. He'd been around enough of them.

Time to go. But he hated to go. "You see any of your old friends?"

"Just Billy. Once. But I met a few kids from here."

"That's good."

He started to get up, then sat back and looked at Freddie.

No, don't.

But he did. "You"—he tried to say it lightly—"you . . . see much of that guy . . . you know, the doctor? Wang?"

"Sometimes."

He felt his heart contract. "I've heard he's a real queer duck."

Freddie looked at him, frowning. "He's—okay."

"You like him?"

"He's—nice."

"You like that guy? You really do?"

"He's okay. He's nice."

He looked at Freddie, trying to tell himself what do you expect a kid to say. Just a kid. The mother brings around someone who's fucking her, what's a kid to say?

But the chink must have bought him something. Kids, it's always the last person who buys 'em something.

"Well . . ." Leon stood up, fighting not to say anything more. "We'd better go."

They walked a few yards, then Leon stopped. "Really. I really heard he's a queer duck. Real queer duck."

Freddie stared at him.

Leon said, suddenly confused, wishing he hadn't said it, "What're you looking at me like that?"

Freddie shook his head quickly.

But there was still that look.

"He bought you something, didn't he?"

Freddie kept staring.

"What'd he buy you? Tell me. He must have bought you something, he's such a great guy. Tell me."

Freddie's eyes brimmed with tears. And the way he was looking at him—like he was crazy.

"What'd he buy you, you think he's so great?"

Freddie was crying. He kept looking around.

"Stop crying!"

But it was ruined, and too late for fixing, and he didn't know what to do, except he wanted to shake him and hit him for ruining it.

Whatever he did for him, bought for him—

Nothing, nothing, nothing meant anything.

"Daddy."

He couldn't help it, he wanted to get away. He was walking far ahead of him now, was fighting not to run. He crossed the street long before him. Then Freddie, crying, ran past him, home.

# 8

LYNN WOKE WITH a little burst of fear, not knowing why until her eyes went to the radio clock on her night table. Ten after nine. Oh, Jesus. She must have forgotten to set it.

Why hadn't Rachel wakened her?

"Rach," she called, stepping into her panties. The silence of the empty house seemed to swallow the sound. Her bra now: the snaps wouldn't catch right away, and one of the shoulder straps had to be untwisted.

Rachel had left a note on the kitchen table in penciled, capital letters—she never used script, and Lynn was tired of trying to make her.

A MAN CALLED YESTERDAY, FORGOT. BEN??? LEN? SORRY. WILL CALL BACK. HAVE A GREAT DAY. LOVE!!!

And under her signature was the moon happy-face she always used.

Mary Hadley, talking to her husband at his desk, looked at her as she walked by toward the stairs. Though Mary said nothing, her eyes under the big brim of her hat were fixed and rebuking.

"Sorry, the damn car," Lynn apologized, and hated herself instantly. For someone who told herself she wasn't all that afraid to lose this job . . . But this was the second morning in a row she was late.

Tina, at the console, waved, then said, "Take your time, it's been pretty slow." But she buzzed her a couple of minutes later. "A Frank Kean. His first time."

"Give me a few seconds." She had to stand up to get a Kleenex from her handbag. She tried to clear that one nostril that often closed up. But she hadn't really needed to, she realized; was just delaying.

She'd probably forgotten a lot of mornings, but it felt even harder this morning to get started. Almost impossible. It had been one of those nights when she'd kept waking in fear that, no matter how cocky she might act in daylight, she was trapped here. And that—a fear she'd been managing to suppress most of the time—Rachel was going to find out.

It was scary that she was even starting to say things, forget things that would give her away.

How could she have forgotten about the cereal boxes?

"Okay," she said to Tina.

A husky voice said, "Hello?"

"Hi. How are you today, Frank?"

"Doing real good. So, your name's Dawn. That's a pretty name, a sexy name. That really your name?"

"Of course." A bird was fluttering near the window. She stood up slightly, trying to make out what it was. It darted away as Frank was saying, "You know, I never done this before. I feel like a nut."

"Why? Why should you feel that way?"

"You know, I'm no kid. I'm fifty-one. I got a wife, I got grown kids. I think—a grown man, doing this. I drive rigs all day, all over the country. So it's not like I don't meet the ladies."

"I'm sure you do."

"But I saw this ad, I thought—hey, I'm curious. So I thought I'd try."

"I'm real glad you did. There's nothing to feel foolish about."

You know where he was? Galveston, Texas. Just outside. In a motel. One of the worst dumps he'd ever been in. But, you see,

80

he'd driven ten hours straight, right through the night, and was going to do four more hours this morning, but wouldn't you know it, his rig broke down. So, here he was in this dump, waiting for it to get fixed.

"You must be exhausted."

"No, I'm all pumped up. Can't sleep. Aggravated about the damn rig."

"That's a shame." She was starting to feel herself settling down a little.

"All goes well, I'm getting out of this business. Three years, I'm gonna pay off the goddam rig and I'm gonna buy us a farm. I got my eye on one in Missouri. Can't take living in rooms and the rig much longer'n that. . . Well," he said. Then, after another pause, "Hey, how about coming over and helping me sleep?"

"Galveston, eh?"

"You know something?" he said quietly. "You've got a nice voice. Tell me what you look like." What would he guess? "I don't know, I'm not good at that."

"Do you like blondes?"

"I've been known to."

"Well, that's what I am. And I'm fairly tall—"

"And you're going to say you've got big tits."

"Why, don't you like them big?"

"Yeah, big and firm. But that's what you always say, right?"

"Frank, I'm sorry, I can't help it, but that's what I've got."

"Got what? Say it."

"I've got nice firm tits. Real big ones."

"And I hope to God you've got a tight ass. My wife, I hate to talk about her, she's hefty in the ass. Never used to be. I hate a fat ass. Can't help it."

"No, I've got a beautiful ass. Guys tell me. And I like to wear real tight jeans."

"Jesus. Do you got much hair there?"

"Do you like a lot?"

"Not real bushy. Is it blonde?"

"Of course."

"Where are you?"

"In my home. In bed."

"You're going to lie to me, but tell me you're gonna take everything off."

"I don't have to lie. There's not much to take off. Just this little thing . . ."

"You're lying."

"Frank, they catch me in a lie, I'm fired."

"What is it you're going to take off?"

"A little negligee . . . Hold on. Just these couple buttons . . . There. That's better. Hi."

After a moment: "You were here, you know what I'd do?"

"Tell me."

"You—like to be eaten?"

"You kidding? What're you trying to do to me?"

"I'd eat you for a week. A week." His voice was changing. "My wife won't let me. Son of a bitch. You know what I want? Tell me to eat you. Beg me. Make believe I won't do it unless you beg me."

"Oh, would I want it. Frank? Frank, honey, eat me. Please, honey, please. Eat me, sweetheart. Come on."

"Your legs open?"

"Are they ever."

"Wide open?"

"Oh, are they."

"For a week. Forever. Except—to fuck you. Eat, fuck—fuck, eat, suck—Open them wider, wider—Fuck, eat . . ."

"Honey, get your tongue in there. Honey, do it, get your tongue in there, work it around, deep . . ."

"I've got it buried. God, is it good. God."

"Deeper, honey. Deeper. Do it deeper."

". . . Oh my," he sighed, after a long moment. "Oh my. I . . ." He let out a breath. "Oh my. Honey, you're something else. You really are. When're you usually on? I want to call you again."

"Generally nine to five."

"I'll call you."

"Please. And good luck with the truck."

And now, less than a minute after Frank hung up, there was Don. And Don, who said he'd never done it before either, said, "Tell me a fantasy—tell me how you'd seduce me, how we'd meet and you'd seduce me." So she told him the easiest one—"Oh, I'm sitting in a bar all alone, and you come in and sit down and I keep looking at you. And after a while we start talking, and I ask would you like to come to my place for a drink. And I bring you the drink, then I start undressing slowly, so slowly . . ." Then after Don there was Tony, who wanted it in a shower, no maybe on the floor, on a shaggy rug. And another Don said he was married, thirty-five, and he'd been with this girl, see, and he'd come with only—you know, a semierection, and ever since then it was that way sometimes with his wife, did you ever hear of it? You did? You think just nerves, the guilts? And Nick, who called her every week, wanted those white, white cheeks opened, tits hanging down. And Gary—

Manya had opened the door quietly, was mouthing the word: lunch? Lynn shook her head; she wanted to make up for coming in late.

—Gary wanted her in a motel, he'd been married nineteen years and had never been in a motel with anyone but his wife. And Josh said, like so many before him, you really are? You're not just saying? And Stepan, here only four months from Russia, and lonely, wanted it in a field somewhere. And afterward there was Tim, then John, and, as her day neared its end, what seemed like HenryMikeLou.


THE FIRST THING Lynn did when she got home was get into a pair of shorts and a loose v-neck blouse and stretch out, barefoot, on one of the lounge chairs on the rear patio. She was too drained to think of cooking or where to go to eat, but she had time, for Rachel was on the phone. She picked up that morning's newspaper, which she hadn't gotten to as yet, glanced at the first three pages, then went to the food section; but after turning a few pages, she wasn't in the mood even for that, and set the paper down.

The air, still bright but with a breeze, carried the smell of honeysuckle, which she loved, from the Hunsickers next door on her left. She might put in honeysuckle on the far end of the lawn, though the gardener who had solicited her for work had said it would make it too "crowded." He'd also advised her to cut down her apple tree, that huge thing of beauty, to give the lawn more light; but she'd rather have the apple tree than a better lawn, and that was the end of him.

She closed her eyes, more to relax with the sun on her face than to try to sleep. All she wanted was this—the sun, the little breeze, the smells. She was startled for a moment by something nuzzling her hand. It was the Hunsicker's toy poodle. She let it lick all around her hand, but when she tried to lift it onto her lap it scampered away and wriggled through the hedge.

Her thoughts began drifting.

To lonely Stepan from Russia. To someone from yesterday— she couldn't remember his name—afraid he was impotent. To Tim from today who couldn't say "words," as he called them, to his wife.

The saved marriages, the rapes that would never happen . . .

Oh, Jesus.

She couldn't believe that even for a half a second she could let herself rationalize it, let herself be Manya, the Hadleys.

"Mother." Rachel was at the back door. "Phone." When Lynn came over, she said quietly, and with a trace of excitement, "I think—the one from yesterday."

Lynn took the call in the kitchen. "Hello."

"Lynn, this is Glenn Norlund. How are you?"

"Just fine. And you?" But it took her until just now to place the name, to remember her neighbor's stepson.

"Am I catching you at the wrong time?"

"No, this is fine."

He was sorry to be calling at the dinner hour, but he was at work and had finally been able to break away to make a call. He'd called yesterday, thinking they might have dinner tonight; and what he was thinking was—if she happened to be free—didn't mind such ridiculous short notice—that maybe she could make it anyway.

She thought. No. "I'm really very sorry. It's got nothing to do with the short notice. I'm just sort of tired and I really can't see getting dressed and going out. Maybe some other—"

Look, he said, then what about this? He hadn't had an evening off in weeks, and had even been feeling a little guilty about taking

84

this one, so what if he brought something over, stayed maybe an hour, an hour and a half, and she could still go to bed early and he could be back at the station by ten-thirty.

"I can bring—pizza? Steak sandwiches? Chinese? Paté de foie gras?"

She looked at her watch. Only a quarter after six.

But why get involved? It was the last thing she needed now. And she certainly didn't need a repeat of the dates she'd had since the divorce—just about all she remembered of them were the hands.

"Hamburgers? Bouillabaisse? Roast goose?"

But maybe it would do her good.


"THAT," GLENN SAID, sitting back from the table, "I would say was good."

"I'm so full." He'd brought too much: two pizzas, a huge hoagie, and a sliced steak sandwich. So Rachel, even though she'd already eaten, had helped out; was back upstairs on the phone with half the hoagie. Lynn said, "Would you like more soda? A drink?"

"No. Nothing." He started to gather up the paper plates and pizza boxes. "No," she said. "Please." But he helped anyway and then washed his hands at the sink, snapping off a paper towel. From the time he'd come in, he gave off the comfortable feeling that he felt at home. In the living room, she sat with her feet tucked under her, while he looked at the small painting of a fisherman she and Jon had picked up at an antique shop. He drifted over to look at a couple of prints. He was tall, maybe six-one; but except for that, and for his eyes, which were a startlingly clear blue, she'd almost forgotten what he looked like. That was a little surprising because he had quite a distinctive face—strong, straight features under loosely swept, light brown hair. He was also a little younger than she remembered, perhaps thirty-six. And surely Rachel would call him preppy—he had on nice beige slacks, cordovan loafers.

"So," he said, sitting down, "it's settled. You're not going to let anyone take away your confidence."

She'd made up a story about why she wanted to leave her

market research job and had told him about her problem finding something else.

"Settled." She smiled, nodded. "And what about you? How are things at the station?"

"It's going to be a long road." Then he smiled. "A challenge, as they say."

He was, as she'd thought his stepmother had said, news director—not a reporter—at Channel 5. He'd been brought in from Detroit to lift its falling ratings; he'd done a similar job at a station there. In fact, though she didn't know if it was Channel 5, she recalled scanning a story in the TV section a few weeks ago about changes at one of the stations, anchors being replaced, reporters shifted around or fired.

It wasn't hard to see him doing that. Though she couldn't see him ever raising his voice, she could picture that face tightening, those eyes narrowing.

"A lot of people didn't like what I was going to do before I even knew what I was going to do," he said. "The thing is, I came in as an enemy to some people right from the beginning. They knew I was here to make some changes. They'd already been raked over by consultants."

What had to be done was try to build on the news staff's strengths while eliminating the weaknesses. Which anchor might be best at what time, who might make good co-anchors? Should you do more multipart stories to try to attract viewers day after day? Should they be four-part stories?—they could drag. Should you change the look of the set? Should sports follow the weather, or weather follow sports?—both could be good at keeping viewers tuned in. Should you cut out editorials, reduce promos?—after all, they take time away from the news.

She said, "I would say you have to know how to make a decision."

He smiled. "Maybe I should have stuck to medicine." Actually med school—he'd dropped out after the first year to become a reporter at a small radio station.

"You mean that?"

"No. Not at all. I realized that just because my father was a doctor was no reason for me to be one."

"How did he feel about that?"

"Whatever I wanted to do. He was quite a guy."

"Was he married to your stepmother then?"

"No, my mother died when I was fourteen, and he didn't marry Liv until a few years ago. He died last year."

"She seems like such a lovely person."

"She really is. Well . . ." He glanced at his watch. "Hey, I enjoyed this."

"Oh, so did I. Are you going back to the station?"

He nodded.

"How late will you stay?"

"Oh . . . after the eleven o'clock news. Twelve. I don't know." He stood up slowly. "Well . . . thank you for letting me come over."

"Thank you. And thanks for the smattering of food."

"If I'd known you ate like a bird."

"Bird. Some bird."

"Is Rachel still up? I'd like to say good night."

She went to the staircase, saw through her partly open door that her light was still on. "Rach."

Rachel came halfway down the stairs. He said, "Rachel, good night. It was real nice meeting you."

"Good night."

She remained standing there as Lynn went with him to the door.

Lynn waited until he got in his car. When she turned, Rachel nodded slowly from the stairs, a certain expression on her mouth. "A fox."

"Not a hunk?"

"They're the same thing."

"Good night, Rachel."

"Good night, Mother," she sang back. She scurried upstairs— and Lynn realized she was still on the phone. Lynn went into the kitchen, washed a few crumbs in the sink into the garbage disposal. Then she just stood there.

It had been such a nice evening.

Gradually, though, she felt herself growing tense.

You've made a mistake. You've put another pair of eyes on you.

# 9

"WHY THE DEVIL wasn't this dressing changed?" Dr. Blay scowled.

Leon, standing next to him at the old man's bedside, looked at him quickly, his face reddening. "I've been busy with 304."

"Well, *someone*." Dr. Blay changed the dressing himself while Leon looked on.

You doctors, you fucking, pompous little gods!

"I want his feet elevated," Dr. Blay said, before he left.

Leon stood staring after him. How had he held himself back? He'd almost gone for that throat.

Where were they, the goddam doctors, at 304? "This man's expired," and the little red-haired shit doctor had put his stethoscope back in his pocket, touched the wife on the arm, mumbled something, and walked out. Where were they when the crying started? He was the one who held her hands while she cried, then held her in his arms and finally led her into a quiet room and sat with her while she sobbed and talked—what a wonderful husband, what a wonderful father, what am I going to do? And he'd stayed with her, letting herself cry herself out, knowing there was no comfort he could give other than being there and letting her know he cared. And all the while his own brain was aflame.

To have left Freddie like that! To just run off like that.

"Lee, lunch?" Maggie approached him with another nurse as he walked back to the nursing station.

"No, I've got some things to do."

Only one thing really, and he didn't know if he should do it.

He took out the phone book and began flipping pages. Then he dialed quickly.

A woman's voice said, "Dr. Wang's office."

"When does he have hours?"

"Here or at the hospital?"

"Both."

After he hung up, he sat staring at the notation, the phone book still open on his lap.

Why did he want to just—get a close look at him? Why?

RACHEL, AFTER GIVING her a kiss, said, "Look what Grandmom sent me."

Lynn, setting down her handbag, looked at the tiny box. It held a pair of shell, pierced earrings.

"They're very beautiful," Lynn said.

"I don't wear pierced *earrings*," Rachel said, almost in disbelief.

"Well . . . don't tell her that. Just write and tell her how beautiful they are."

"Pierced *earrings*," Rachel said, shaking her head.

"Did she write anything?"

Rachel showed her a note, which said that the instant she'd seen these she had thought of Rachel; she hoped she and her mother were doing well, and signed it "lovingly." The earrings were so typical of Jon's mother. She'd moved from Baltimore to a retirement village in Florida, and every few months she would send Rachel a little gift, generally something just as frivolous, such as a picture frame made of coral. It was as if she wanted to think that Rachel had everything else; that she didn't want to know, which she did as of five, six months ago, that Jon rarely sent any money. It was the kind of thinking Lynn had seen from the time Jon had brought her home to meet her. A widow, very imperious-looking and intimidating to Lynn, who lived on what Jon called

90

the "remnants of old family money." She'd wanted them to consider buying a house as soon as they got married. Somehow it didn't seem to register that Lynn would be giving up college and getting a job, that they'd have to live in Jon's efficiency.

Lynn changed into shorts and went into the kitchen to see what she could make for dinner that wouldn't take too long: she *had* to clean this house tonight. Yes, Rachel called from upstairs, stir-fried chicken was fine; so Lynn cut the chicken breasts she had into nuggets, heated up peanut oil in her wok, and slid in the chicken and some Chinese vegetables. As she watched it sizzle and smoke, she could feel the anxieties of the day begin to drain away.

Later, while Rachel cleaned the kitchen, she started in the living room, dusting, running the vacuum sweeper behind the sofa, pulling aside chairs, lamp tables. She used to have a cleaning woman come in once a week, but had let her go a couple months before the divorce became final.

Carrying the sweeper upstairs, Lynn vacuumed the hall, the bedrooms. She'd made up her mind she wasn't going to change the linens tonight, but suddenly she wanted to, wanted to turn the mattresses. Rachel came up to help, but Lynn only had her do her closet and the hall closet, while she did the bathrooms. She scrubbed the tile floors, the tubs, the stall showers, each thing seeming to lure her to the next.

She was in bed by ten-thirty, having soaked for a long while in the tub. She felt achy, tired—but cleansed of almost every thought. She wanted to read the paper, watch some TV, sleep. But the paper had more than the usual grim news—another terrorist bombing, an even bigger story of a man who confessed killing and mutilating four housewives . . . She turned to the help-wanted section.

She felt the mattress sag next to her. She hadn't heard Rachel come into the room.

"Good night, Mom."

"Good night, sweetheart." She brought Rachel to her and kissed her.

"Mom?" Rachel seemed hesitant to leave. "Is anything wrong?"

She was startled by the question. "No. Why?"

"I don't know. You—sometimes look worried."

"No, I'm not worried. I may just get tired now and then."

"You know something? Some day I'm going to be so rich I'm going to give you everything you could ever want. I'm going to be president of—some big company. I'm going to sit at one of those big tables with water pitchers and people around it who work for me—"

"Hey, I can see it now. And what will your husband do?"

"I don't know. I haven't thought about a *husband.*"

"Well, what about thinking about going to sleep? It's getting late. Good night, sweetheart."

"Night, Mom."

Lynn watched her walk off, a little stunned. She hadn't realized that her worry came through. She had to do something. And fast. But this wasn't the way, getting anxious again.

She clicked on the TV, gave a situation comedy a try, then found a documentary about the Antarctic that was relaxing. She watched it, then the beginning of the news. She kept it on while she reached for one of her *Gourmets.* She was reading when she heard something that drew her attention. She looked up and saw people picketing an adult bookstore somewhere.

She watched for a moment, then turned back to the magazine. Then she looked up again, quickly.

It was just a little jolt to see that it was on Channel 5.

IT GREW DARK as he sat watching Wang's house—a large, stone row house—from his car. For the past couple hours people had been drifting in and out. But his office hours should be over soon. Still, that didn't mean he would be coming out. He probably lived upstairs.

Leon straightened a little as a man walked down the front steps. It was hard to tell in the light from the few street lamps, and from this distance four houses away, if he was Chinese. But he was coming this way, and Leon saw he wasn't.

Yesterday he'd sat outside the hospital for three hours, hoping just to get a good look at his face. Nothing more, just that. Now there was something pumping inside him.

He'd only gotten a fast glimpse that one time he'd seen him with Della. And he had to see it up close—the face that stole Della, that stole Freddie. That ruined everything. Even his one last chance with Freddie.

That couple? Could it be him with Della?

No.

That one? No, a woman and a kid.

Then no one at all.

Until, about an hour later, a man walked down the steps, holding a small dog on a leash. The dog scampered around, then paused to squat, sniffed at the sidewalk, went to the left, the right. The man—it seemed to be—it seemed to be—yes, he was Chinese—was coming this way, stopping every so often to let the dog sniff the ground.

Leon pressed himself low in the seat. But he could make out Wang's round face, glasses, what seemed like a little smile on his lips.

The bastard smiling!

Leon whirled around as Wang passed the car. He watched him through the rear window. He'd stopped again as the dog sniffed near the curb. The dog started to tug him into the street, but Wang held it back. He was standing at the corner now.

Now he was coming back.

Leon watched. The chink was smiling down at his fucking dog. He watched him coming closer, his heart rocketing.

Whatever the dog did, he smiled.

That fucking smile. Hello, Freddie, and he must smile. Look what I got for you, Freddie, and the smile. Probably he even smiled when he fucked.

Why shouldn't he smile?

Had everything, took everything—

Leon stared at him as he slowly walked by. He was barely aware that his hand had moved up to the door handle. All at once he flung open the door and was on the sidewalk, punching Wang on the back of his neck and the side of his face. As he fell, he kicked him in the chest, the face, down in the crotch, then up in the face again. Kicked him for Della, for Freddie, for all the shit he'd ever taken.

Then, as Wang lay hunched over on the ground, his hands to his face, the dog yapping, something told him to grab his wallet.

HE PULLED INTO his driveway, then sat slumped against the wheel. His heart boomed up at him.

Why had he done it? Why hadn't he controlled himself? They could be coming after him. Wang might have seen his face, or he might have dropped something.

He sat looking at the wallet. He'd grabbed it, hoping they'd think it was a mugger.

He was lucky he hadn't had his gun.

If he got out of this, he'd go see someone he could trust. Maybe Irv, the psychologist he'd nursed. He wouldn't be like a psychologist, but a friend. Yes. Maybe he'd go.

He lifted his face slowly and stared out at the street.

But who he really needed was her.

# 10

THE NEXT MORNING, on his way to work, Leon drove over to an all-night luncheonette to buy a morning paper. Back in the car he scanned it quickly, then looked at each page carefully. It hadn't really hit him until the middle of the night that maybe he'd killed him. Even if he'd hurt him seriously it would have been in here, wouldn't it?

He drove off and, after he had gone a block, slowed down and dropped the paper in a trash can. It had almost felt like a piece of evidence against him.

About fifteen minutes later, only a few miles from the hospital, he saw the police car.

He hadn't been sure at first, in the gray light of early morning, but there it was, like the solid nose of a shark about a half block behind him.

He shot a quick look at the speedometer. He was only going thirty, and it was a thirty-five mile speed limit. So it wasn't that. Still, he eased up on the gas ... Was the police car slowing up too? His eyes kept going from the rearview mirror to the sideview mirror. There was a sudden tumult in his chest.

He was sure of it. But if they wanted him, why didn't they just do it? Why hadn't they come to his house? Why were they just following him?

Three blocks away was the street leading to the hospital. He turned at the intersection, a drumming in the back of his head. He forced himself to stare straight ahead, didn't look back until he drove into the parking lot. No one was behind him. He pulled into a spot and looked again, in all directions. He couldn't see a police car, but maybe it came in during the few moments he hadn't been looking.

"Morning, Lee."

He turned, startled. Maggie was smiling at him near his window.

"Ready for another day?" she said.

"I guess."

He never realized she talked so much. About her toddler, and how guilty she felt leaving him all day with a lady, but what could you do, she and her husband needed the two salaries. And then about private duty, did he ever do private duty? No, he didn't think he'd like that. Well, she'd been thinking about it, working private duty nights and being with the boy during the day. Then when he was in first grade, maybe even kindergarten, she might still work nights and go for her masters during the day.

On the floor, he went off to the men's room and wet his face, rubbing cold water on his forehead and his eyes. At the nursing station, he sat down with some charts to go over the last shift's notes. He still felt a little shaken.

"Mr. Owens," a student nurse said, holding out the phone; he hadn't heard it buzz.

"Owens," he said.

"Lee, Dorothy." It was the director of nurses. "Could I see you, please?"

Hanging up, he sat frozen. The police? Take him away in front of everyone?

But she immediately smiled when he entered the office, lifting her massive body from behind the desk and holding out her hand.

"Let me congratulate you, Lee. You're one of the nominees for Nurse of the Year."

He stared at her. Every year the nurses were asked to name

96

three nurses and to give the reasons for their choices. The winner was then selected by the administration, and was honored at a dinner.

Compassionate. Gives freely of his time.

These, she said, still smiling, were just some of the good things said about him.

He kept staring. Him? Didn't they know he didn't deserve it?


MANYA CAME INTO Lynn's office first thing in the morning to say she wouldn't be able to go out to lunch with her; but she and Louise were going to have dinner together after work—could she make it?

"Gosh, I'm sorry. I can't."

"O-kay. Some other time."

Lynn felt a little uncomfortable. It was the second time Manya had asked. She hated for Manya to sense it, didn't know what to do if she asked again, but the truth was she wanted to leave everything about this world behind once she walked out the door.

"Lynn," Tina said, "can I see you for a second?"

She handed her a page and a half of names and addresses of men who had called yesterday. There were question marks next to several of them. Tina had been so busy she had neglected to mark down who had talked to them, and she needed it for commissions.

Lynn wrote her name next to two of them, continued looking down the list. She stopped all at once.

The first image that sprang into her mind was of two towheaded boys, then a beautiful blonde mother and a handsome young father.

George Pastori?

Her neighbor, George *Pastori*?


HE TRIED LOSING himself in the paperwork he hated.

It panicked him, all the people who'd been coming up to the nursing station to congratulate him. Nurses. Doctors. Even some of the patients, their families.

Hey, Lee, just heard.

No one deserves it more.

Don't know what my mother would do without you.

But if they knew just one of the things about him. About the little girl. Almost killing that blonde from the bar. About the chink. He didn't want any award, praise, didn't want to be up on a dais, didn't want all these faces coming close, the big smiles, the handshakes, the eyes. The only one he wished he could tell was Della. Not that she would care, but he wanted her to know, to tell Freddie. That there were people in this world who liked him, thought he was something, that Freddie had a good father, that he wasn't crazy.

But how could he call after what he did to Freddie?

At coffee break he went to a pay phone, drawn by a sudden sense of urgency. He dialed her hospital number.

"I want to talk to Della Owens. A nurse."

But she wasn't on her unit. Would he like her paged?

"Yes."

About a minute later, "Della Owens."

"Della, Leon."

For a moment he thought she'd hung up. Then, "How dare you call."

"Dell, please. Just this. Tell Freddie—I'm sorry."

"You're crazy, you know?"

"Just tell him." Don't say any more, he thought, just hang up. But he said it. "I—was nominated for an award." It came out so weakly he was ashamed. "Nurse of the Year."

"Oh Christ," she said wearily. "You do fool the world, don't you?"

And hung up.

He stood there a while, his heart going wildly. Then he began pushing coins in the phone.

"I want to talk to Dawn. This is Wing."

"Could you call back—say, ten minutes?"

"Is she there?"

"She's on another call."

Hanging up, he propped a hand against the wall, stared down

at his feet. This wasn't the first time he'd had to call back, but it had become torture to think of her talking to someone else.

TINA HAD SAID it was Wing. Lynn's hand hovered over the phone. Finally she picked it up.

"Dawn?"

"Yes." Her skin had prickled when she heard his name.

He hesitated. "I—just want you to know I'm sorry. About last time. I'd had something to drink and I really don't drink. So I want you to know I'm sorry. Okay?"

"Okay." She felt some of her tension leaving.

"And I wanted to tell you something. I just got some good news and I wanted to tell you. I—just won an award."

"Really?"

"They just told me. It's for helping people."

"Congratulations, that's wonderful. You must feel very good."

"I just wanted to tell you."

"I'm really happy for you."

"I just wanted you to know," he said awkwardly.

"I'm glad you did. That's really wonderful. Congratulations again."

"I've been trying to call you. I wanted to tell you. But you've been on the phone. You get lots of calls, don't you?"

"I've been pretty busy, yes."

"Well, I just wanted to tell you." He hesitated again. "I don't want anything else. Just wanted to tell you."

"I'm really happy for you."

"All—all I wish I could do was just—hold you. You hold me. That's all." There was a long silence; he apparently wanted the silence. Then he said, "That's all, that was all. I—didn't do anything . . . So—I'll talk to you, okay?"

"Fine."

"So I'll talk to you again," he said.

She hung up slowly; felt a little dazed. In its own way it was even stranger than his last call.

# 11

AS LYNN NEARED her house and saw the Pastoris' van in their driveway, the thought hit her: what if she'd been the one, not Louise, Tina had given his call to? Even though Tina would have told her his name first, what if she'd taken the call absentmindedly? Or if Tina had mispronounced the name?

Still, that was only part of what jolted her at seeing his name. Maybe even the smallest part. The biggest was—just that he'd called. She'd even almost asked Louise about it, but somehow that would have been obscene, wrong.

In her driveway she started to reach for the remote to raise the garage door but then remembered she was supposed to drive Rachel and Tiffany to the movies.

Rachel called to her from upstairs when she walked in. "Hi. Hey, Mom, you know Tracy?"

"No, she's only in here three times a week."

Rachel came downstairs. "She's having a nose job."

"Really? I never saw anything wrong with her nose."

"You didn't? You didn't? She got a little bump. Right here."

"I never noticed."

"The doctor's going to make believe it's a deviated something-or-other, so's Blue Cross or something will pay for it."

"I ought to call her parents and have them tell her more secrets."

"Oh, Mom. I'm her friend."

Lynn smiled. "So what's this about a movie? When are you going?"

"It starts at seven. Mom, can I make dinner? Omelets? Do we have mushrooms?"

"Look in the closet." She started upstairs. "Do you know when I pick you up?"

"Ten-thirty?" She said it hesitantly.

Lynn looked at her. "From seven to ten-thirty? It's three and a half hours?"

"We want to see the beginning again."

"You're not going to see the beginning again. Or let Tiffany's mother pick you up if you want to see the beginning again."

In her room, changing, she thought: Friday, thank God. She remembered that she'd promised to call her friend Nan Voelmer this week, and wondered should she do it this evening. But she really wasn't up to it. Maybe she would go to that little place in the mall, where she and Rachel had seen a blouse that Rachel had decided against but wanted now. But all those people. . .

On top of everything, her period felt this close.

"Mom," Rachel called from downstairs, "where?"

"Where what?"

"The mushrooms."

"Did you look in the closet? That's where they are."

"I *looked*."

"Well, look again. Take your time."

Standing by one of the windows, she could see the Pastoris' van through a slight opening in the curtain, thought of George hosing it down yesterday in preparation for their trip, the boys dancing under the spray in their swim trunks.

Impulse? Had it been that? Just—curiosity? Or, like so many, wanted words? Wanted lights, not the dark? Someone fat? Skinny? Tall? . . .

"It was in back," Rachel called.

102

As Lynn started downstairs, the phone rang. She took it in her room. Glenn. Was he interrupting dinner?

"No, not at all, we haven't started yet."

Was she free to go out tomorrow night?—he'd love to see her.

She said, "Let me see what Rachel's doing. I really hate to leave her alone."

Walking downstairs, she felt a little frightened, a part of her wishing that Rachel would tell her she had no one to be with.

But Rachel, standing at the stove, said sure—Tiffany'd either come here or she'd go there.

"MY BROTHER," TIFFANY whispered excitedly into the phone the next morning, "is a pervert."

Tiffany's brother, who was fifteen, could very well be. He was always reading.

"Can you hear me?" Tiffany whispered.

"Yesss."

"I was in his room and found—snajorts."

It took just a moment to figure out, even though their secret language didn't always follow the same rules, and they hadn't used it since they were maybe nine. Rachel said, "Gross." And meant it. Trojans.

"And irdy ixtures of eople ooing dit."

Dirty pictures, *doing* it? "That's gross." But this time she giggled. Tiffany began giggling too. Rachel said, "Did you tell him?"

"You *queer?* He'd kill me."

It *was* gross—but Rachel kept thinking of it for a little while after she hung up: not just *what* Tiffany said, but what the pictures might look like, what a Trojan—even the *box*—looked like up close. She thought about telling her mother—she could talk to her about almost anything—but this really was gross.

She went downstairs, where her mother was putting away a load of things she'd just brought back from the supermarket. She didn't notice that Rachel had come into the kitchen.

No matter what her mother said, she did seem worried, especially now, when she didn't know anyone was looking.

"Mom."

Lynn turned. "Oh."

"Let me help you."

"No, there's only room for one."

"Why didn't you tell me you were going shopping?"

"Oh, you were sleeping."

"But I told you to wake me if you were going."

Her mother put several more cans away, then turned again. "Tiffany's definitely coming over?"

"Yes."

"Early?" Glenn had called again and said he'd like to pick her up in the afternoon.

"Yep."

She kept looking at her mother. She hated to lie—Tiff was going out with her family—but she wanted her mother to go.

LET'S TAKE AN old-fashioned Sunday drive, Glenn had said—go out to the country somewhere and get lost. What a nice way it was of getting lost, Lynn thought: a beautiful day, farmland all around, a BMW with a new car smell, the sun roof open. She could feel herself starting to relax for the first time since they'd left her house: Masters was a thousand miles away, there was no Wing, no Ray, no Don, no Sid, no doubts about herself, what she was going to do. Even Glenn had become much less intimidating to her, had become just a nice guy handling a pressure job.

And apparently, after two calls to the station as they drove, he was just starting to really relax too.

He smiled. "So. You were a tomboy."

"Did I say that?"

"You said that."

"Oh—I liked to climb roofs and beat up boys. But I liked to play *jacks*. And I had a doll. It smoked a cigar, but I had a doll."

He grinned, shot her a look across his shoulder. She said, "Look at that."

Two horses, sleek chestnuts, were streaking across a field, would stop to nuzzle each other and wrestle with their manes, then streak away again. In the distance was a scattering of cattle on a hill.

Glenn said, "Let me let this guy go by. I'm going too slow for him."

104

He drew to the side of the narrow road, and a car that had been tailgating them whizzed by. The road twisted through patches of woods, then opened up to a long stretch of farmland again.

"So," she said, "you haven't told me."

"Told you what?"

"I don't know. Did you like to climb roofs?"

No. Trees, he used to be big on trees. In fact, the first thing he remembered ever wanting to be was a forest ranger. Then that became a lot of other things, then finally a doctor, then really finally a reporter. Actually, he'd always assumed he would remain a reporter, but one of the station managers he worked for felt he would make a good news director, which led to a job at a somewhat larger station, then a larger one, then the one in Detroit. No, he didn't do any actual reporting anymore. His work involved supervising a lot of people, planning stories, hiring and firing. . .

"I like Lorna Finch," she said. "Did you hire her?"

"Yes, I knew her in Detroit. She only anchored on weekends there. She's very good."

"She really is."

Hey, look at that, he said suddenly. Just ahead, at a turn in the road, was a creek. People were gliding along in rubber rafts and large inner tubes. He drove along the road bordering the creek.

"That looks like an awful lot of fun," she said.

"Ever do it?"

"No. You?"

"When I was a kid." He pulled to the side, stopped. A young couple, their legs dangling over the tube, held up beers to them. Lynn waved. He said, "A vow. Someday we're going to come back with bathing suits."

"A vow."

He pulled onto the road. "Mark this creek well. Do you know where we are?"

"No."

"Well, remember this tree. It has leaves on it. Now what would really be nice right now is a little place to eat that was built, say, in eighteen, well, eighteen-twenty, has the original beams, a water wheel."

"And called Ye Olde Water Wheel."

"Ye olde something. Ye olde anything."

"I'm afraid," she said shortly, "we're coming out of the country."

"And I'm afraid you're right."

They were passing estates, then scattered clusters of houses.

"Where," he said, looking for road signs, "are we?"

"Oh, I know where we are now," she said.

"You do? Oh, damn it."

"THAT," LYNN SAID, "couldn't have been better. I don't think I've ever had it better."

And she wasn't just saying it. Everything—the mussels, the salad, the clams linguine, even the *bread,* she didn't know where they got this bread—was just right.

"Are you sure no dessert?"

"No, no. I'm sure."

"A drink?"

"No, the wine was—" She held up her hands; absolutely nothing more.

"This was quite a find."

"Wasn't it?" Luck. It had just looked inviting.

She looked at him as he went over the check. It was an even stronger face in the light of the candle, more intense.

Two of the growing multitude, she thought—the divorced.

In the car she said again, "That was so good."

"Wasn't it?"

And she felt good, was pleasantly tired.

As they turned into her driveway she felt a sudden, surprised beating in her chest. Please, she thought, don't let him ruin it with hands. Parked, he shifted around to look at her. "Well, it was really beautiful. And I thank you."

"Thank you."

He leaned over and kissed her quickly, then held his hand briefly on her cheek. He kept looking at her. Then he slid out and opened her door.

# 12

---

MAYBE, LEON THOUGHT in sudden panic, he ought to just drive away and call Irv from somewhere and say he'd gotten sick or that everything was all right now and he didn't need to see him after all.

He stared at the house, a rancher, from the curb. Lights were on in the living room; someone's shadow passed briefly across the thin drapes. Irv's office was on the side, a lantern glowing over the entrance. A separate path, lighted softly at foot level, led up to it. On the lawn near the sidewalk was the sign: Dr. Irving Goldstein, Psychologist.

One thing for sure, he thought. No matter what he decided to do now, no way would he come here during the day. Not with that sign, telling everyone in the neighborhood that whoever walked up there was a nut.

Maybe that was why Irv even gave him an appointment at night.

That would be Irv.

"Hey, good to hear from you," Irv had said on the phone. "Been meaning to call you."

One friend to another.

"Lee," he'd told him at the hospital, "I'll never forget you. You've saved my sanity."

So, it wasn't like he'd be seeing a shrink. A regular shrink.

But, though he got out of the car, it was still a while before he could break from it and walk up the path. A little sign on the door said Ring. He finally pressed the buzzer, and Irv's voice came over the intercom. "Yes?"

"It's Lee."

"Be with you shortly, Lee," and there was a buzz and he opened the door. He walked into the waiting room. No one else was there. He sat down at one end of an orangy imitation-leather couch that seemed to engulf him, wondered should he take one of the chairs. The door to Irv's office was closed. He could hear the faint sound of a TV from the house.

His heart was still beating fast, but not, he thought, as fast as before.

He didn't know what all he would tell him. There was so much. About Della and Freddie and the chink, about—if he could bring himself to—the little girl, and all about Dawn, which seemed even harder to talk about than the little girl. The little girl, he'd never do that again, but Dawn, he didn't know how to stop himself. Or if he even wanted to.

"There's no one I can talk to," Irv had said, crying, the day after his colostomy. "People think, a psychologist, I don't need help."

"Or maybe," Leon remembered saying, reaching down and touching his hand, "that's all in your head. Maybe you think because you're a psychologist you shouldn't need help."

And Irv had looked at him in a kind of amazement. And he began letting out his fears, some of which his doctor may have assumed he'd reassured him about: that maybe his wife wouldn't want to have sex with him now that he had to wear a bag, that he'd always smell, that he wouldn't be able to live any kind of normal life any more.

"Lee, you're better than any psychologist or psychiatrist," he'd said.

The door to Irv's office was opening now, and Irv followed a man out. Leon looked at Irv, thinking Irv would say hello right away to him. But Irv's eyes stayed on the man until he reached the door. "I'll see you next week," he said. And only then did he turn. "Lee," and he held out his hand.

Irv let Leon walk in first, then closed the door. He said, "Why don't you sit here, and I'll sit here."

Leon sat down. He'd been off the day Irv was discharged, and the last time he'd seen him he had been in a hospital gown for some reason, not his pajamas—a skinny, balding little man, in a gown with the back open, who was always hesitant about standing up straight. Now he was wearing a gray, lightweight suit, was deeply tanned. He stood by his desk briefly, looking at something, his body straight, then came over and sat near Leon in an identical deep, leather chair. He didn't, as Leon thought he might, take off his jacket.

"You look well," Irv said. There seemed to be a touch of surprise in his voice, as if he hadn't expected it of someone who wanted to see him.

Leon nodded. He was beginning to feel as anxious as he had been outside. Though he wanted to ask Irv how he'd been doing this past year, if all the things they'd talked about had worked out all right, he found he couldn't bring himself to.

"So," Irv said, "tell me what's been happening in your life."

"Oh . . ." But he was dismissing every fragment of a thought that came into his head. Irv was sitting back, his arms folded on his chest, legs crossed. Behind him, on the walnut-paneled wall, were three diplomas.

"Just take it easy," Irv said. "Try to relax."

Leon took a breath. "Well—I'm separated from my wife." He waited, thinking Irv might say something like I'm sorry. Something. When he didn't he said, "She has the boy."

"I didn't know you had a son," he said.

Because I never talked about myself, Leon thought; I was always listening. "Yes. He's ten." But he couldn't think of where to go with it.

"What happened?"

"Why we got separated?"

"Yes."

He shrugged. Then he leaned forward, elbows on his knees. He looked at the floor. "She had a boyfriend. Still does." He stopped.

Still looking at the floor, he heard Irv say quietly, "Try to tell me."

Well, she has this boyfriend. A Chinaman, a doctor she works with. But even though she has a boyfriend, she's still allowed to keep the boy, and he isn't even allowed to see him.

His eyes filled. He looked up. "She's the one—she's the one screwing around—I can't see the boy. Anything like that? You ever hear?"

"But why? I don't understand."

"That's a damn good question. She's screwing around, the boy has to see a psychiatrist—I'm the one they blame. You ever hear anything like that?"

"What do you mean they blame you? Why?"

"You should hear her. 'Everyone thinks he's so good, so nice. They don't know his temper.' *Temper*. I was just told—I'm up for Nurse of the Year." He looked at Irv, but Irv didn't show any reaction. "Temper! And because I bought him a lot of things. I wanted the best for him, so I bought him a bike—what's wrong with a bike? A radio. I bought him a lot of things. A rifle. I wouldn't let him keep it in his room, anything like that, I kept it. I thought we'd go target shooting. But she made such a big deal. And a motorbike." The tears were spilling over. He wiped them away with the back of his hand. "I wanted him to have things, what's the big crime?"

When he didn't go on, Irv said, "And you haven't seen him at all?"

"Oh—once."

"How did that come about? I thought you weren't allowed to."

"Oh—she let me. Big, big favor."

Irv said, after another wait, "How did it go?"

"Oh." He looked down again. He couldn't bring himself to go into that yet. He'd have to tell him about walking away from him, and no one, not even Irv, would understand. "It was okay."

"Do you think maybe she will let you see him again?"

He shrugged. When he looked up, finally, during a long stretch of silence, he saw Irv in that same position, arms crossed, leg crossed. It—was so different. So different from those times he used to sit by Irv's bed . . . It's not going to change your sex life at all, Irv. You listen to me, Irv. You're going to be fine, Irv.

Irv said, "Lee, you haven't told me—and I've been hoping it

110

would just come up as we talked—what you'd like me to help you with."

Leon felt his face redden. He said, in confusion, "I don't know—maybe help me get her back, the boy."

"Would she come in here with you?"

"I don't know."

"Did she ever want you to go with her for counseling?"

"It was more like—'You need a psychiatrist.' You know, like I was the one. She even got my mother on me. Everyone believes her, that's the thing. Everything she says."

"But did she ever suggest the two of you going?"

He was staring down again. "Maybe. I think. I don't know. Once."

In that same quiet voice: "Did you ever go?"

Leon's head shot up. "Why should I? I wasn't the one! And if I did, he'd only believe her. I tell you, everyone believes her."

"Believes what? Would you give me an example?"

"Whatever she says!" He couldn't understand that damn question—he'd already told him. "My temper, whatever I did was wrong."

"Lee, what about this business of a temper? Did she say, for instance, that you hit her?"

"Hit her. Everything."

"Did you ever hit her?"

He tried to work out what to say. If he told him four or five times, he'd think they were really hits when they were only slaps. The only real time was that night of the hearing. "Once. One night I finally told her I knew about her running around, and she came at me and I hit her."

"Can I ask why, if you knew all along, you never said anything before?"

What could he say? That he was scared to lose her because of Freddie but mostly, mainly, because she was the only one he'd ever been able to screw? That though it wasn't good any more, that even though he was back to popping off and not even that, it used to be good—and that that was enough? That he was scared to start out again? How do you say that to a guy looking at you with his arms crossed? "I just didn't, that's all."

"Do you have any idea why you did that night?"

111

Now he'd have to tell him about Della yelling at him after the hearing, and Irv would say what hearing—And he couldn't tell him about the little girl either, not yet anyway. "I—just did," he said.

"I'm trying to understand something. You hit her that one time. Is that why she said you had such a temper? Or did you used to have a lot of quarrels?"

What was this? He'd just told him he'd hit her—what was this about quarrels? What was he trying to get at? Leon glared at him. "You know, I may have blown up once or twice. I blew up once or twice. But someone keeps saying, 'You're wrong, you should have done this, that,' you blow up. Christ."

"I'm trying to get as much of the picture as I can, Lee." After another pause he said, "How did you get along sexually?"

His face grew hotter. This wasn't just a question. This wasn't just how did you get along. It was, You got along lousy, didn't you? It was, This was why the quarrels, why the boyfriend. It was, What did you expect?

"Okay."

"No problems?"

"No." He'd just said okay, didn't he? Didn't he?

"I'd like to go back to your last meeting with your son."

This too? He'd already told him that it went okay.

Irv said, "You really didn't say much about it. Did it go all right?"

What was he looking for? Why didn't he just believe him? When Irv was in that fucking hospital gown, all bent over, had he ever said Irv, what're you really crying about—your mother didn't give you candy as a kid? Did he? Did he? He'd said Irv, cry, let it all out, I'm here, I'm your friend. And he'd held his hand—he hadn't sat there with his fucking arms crossed.

"It went all right. I told you."

"But you looked upset."

Look at him looking at him. Like Sherlock Holmes.

"It was just the boyfriend—" Here he was saying it, and he didn't want to, because then he'd have to say about wanting to hit Freddie and then just wanting to get away. And she'd be right again.

"What about the boyfriend, Lee?"

112

"He said he likes the Chinaman, loves him."

"He said that? Loves him?"

Again like he didn't believe him! And after this he'd go back to how was your sex life, and did you really only hit her once, digging, probing—

Suddenly the big shot. A big shot with a shit bag on him!

"How did he come to say that?"

Leon stared at him. "What do you mean, how he said that?"

"I mean, what was the context? What brought it on?"

"What do you mean what brought it on? What're you driving at? Whatever I say you want me to say something else. You don't believe a damn thing I say. What're you looking for? Tell me!"

"I'm just trying to help."

"Help? Is this the kind of help I gave you when you needed help? I came to a friend, I wanted a friend, I don't want any goddam Sigmund Freud. Why weren't you Sigmund Freud in the hospital?"

Irving Goldstein's face went red, but he said nothing.

"I've got to go!" He was on his feet.

"Lee, don't—"

"I've got to go. I want to go."

And don't try to stop him!

He was doing this again—maybe would regret it—but don't try to stop him!

# 13

MANYA TAPPED ON Lynn's door, then opened it. "Hon, you free a couple minutes?"

"I can be."

Manya, in tangerine slacks and a frilly blouse, her hair in its usual coiffed bubble, half-sat on the edge of Lynn's desk.

"Hon, don't take this wrong, but I have to do it—I got a call. You remember a Bill Fergus?"

Lynn thought, then shook her head.

"Called you yesterday?"

Still unable to remember—how could you remember them all?—she started to reach for her file box. Manya motioned that it wasn't necessary. "He just called, wanted to speak to the boss, Tina put me on. Hon, he's probably a crank, I'm sure he is, but I've got to tell you. He said you brushed him off very quickly, that it was like you couldn't wait to get rid of him."

"I don't remember."

"Look, it happens. But I had to tell you. In fact, Hadley wants everything like this reported to him, but I wouldn't—"

"Then do it."

"Hon, don't get angry at me. Please. Someone may call him some day. I just have to let you know."

"I'm sorry, it's a little upsetting."

"Listen, you can't do this all day like you're making your big debut at the Met. I know that. That's why we have the cards. Do you use them?"

"Now and then." Never, lately.

"I still have to use them now and then, and I wrote 'em. So look," she said, standing up with a smile. She didn't finish. At the door she said, "I was really thinking of you."

"I know."

"See you."

"I'll see you."

But she was still angry. Angry that Manya had come in with it, couldn't wait until after work or when they happened to meet in the washroom. And upset at herself because it worried her.

It especially worried her today because of another interview she'd gone out on at lunch. A combination copywriter-secretarial job, but she'd had the feeling when she left that they wanted someone younger, someone they felt would be completely happy with an "entry level" salary, as they called it.

Still, she promised herself she wasn't going to let the call affect her; but when the next call came, she was aware how she was focusing her full self on it.

"It's me again—Frank. Guy that drives a rig? Remember?"

"Of course I remember you." She had just looked up his card, after Tina buzzed. "How are you?"

"Not too bad. Just had lunch. Two dogs with chili. Shouldn't have had the chili. Got a sore throat and it sort of burns."

"Oh, I'm sorry."

"You know where I am? Just outside Charleston, South Carolina. You ever been to Charleston?"

"No, never."

"Pretty town. One of the prettiest I ever seen."

"You staying there overnight?"

"No, I'm going to Chattanooga. I like Chattanooga okay. I like most towns okay, though mostly you just drive through a town, or if you stop you don't really get to see much. I'm going to Topeka tomorrow. But I don't want to go through Missouri. I got my eye on a farm there, maybe I told you, I think I did, but I got my eye on

116

a farm there when I quit this. But I don't like driving through Missouri. The bears—you know, the state cops?—they're so tough if you go over the limit we call Missouri 'misery.' You know, Missouri? Misery? . . . Hey, I told my old lady about you."

"Really?"

"Yeah, I said I called a certain number from a motel, and I got this sweet little gal. She said, 'You're lying.' I said, 'I'm not lying.' She said, 'What did she say?' I said, 'Oh, she told me her name's Dawn, she got big breasts.' She said, 'She told you she got big breasts?' I said, 'Fact is, she told me she got big tits.' 'She told you she got big tits? She actually used that word?' I said, 'Yeah.' She said, 'What else did she say?' . . . Dawn, honey I don't know she believes me or not, but I had myself a good time that night, I never saw her hotter. When I started thinking what if she goes through my Visa bill—she never does, but what if she does—I figured out a pretty good excuse. But I was thinking maybe I won't even need one—you know, what it did for her. . . Anyway, so. How're you doing?"

"Good, really good."

"So, you never been to Charleston? Do I wish you were here. You know what I'd do if you were here? I'd show you the houses. You'd think you were back in the Civil War, before the Civil War. The gardens, they got pretty gardens. They got something called the Battery, you walk along the water—really something. And then we'd come back to the motel. Or the rig. You ever do it in a rig?"

"No."

"Not much of a bed for two up in back of the seat. So, how about the seat? Gotta be careful of the steering wheel though, the gear shift—that's okay?"

"Okay."

"You'll put one leg up near the gear shift? The other up against the door? Nice and wide?"

"I've got them real wide."

"Honey, I'm beginning to fall in love with you . . ."

But it came across as part of the game, and not with the intensity of Wing, who called shortly before she was to leave.

"Yes, Wing."

117

"Dawn, I want you to tell me something. Would you tell me what you really look like? And don't say, what do you think I look like or what would you like me to look like."

"But that's what you've wanted."

"I know, but tell me. Really tell me."

She didn't have to think, gave the usual description. "I'm five-five, slender, with long blonde hair."

"What do you mean long? How long?"

"Oh, it comes just below my shoulders."

"And your eyes. What color are your eyes? Really tell me."

"They're blue."

"And how old are you, really?"

"Twenty-eight."

"Can I ask how come you're not married?"

She'd told him she was single, because it was one of the rules—unless the client wanted you to be married. She said, "I don't know. I haven't thought much about it."

"Dawn?"

"Yes."

"Just once? Only once? Say at a restaurant—lots of people. Wherever there'd be lots of people. I'd never say meet me where we're alone. I'd never say that."

"Wing, I told you, I can't. I'm not allowed to."

"I don't think you'd be ashamed. People say—I'm not bad-looking."

"I'm sure of it. But I'm not allowed to."

"And I wouldn't try anything. I swear. Even the last time we talked, I never said anything like do something to me or let me do something to you. I just wanted to talk to you. And I just want to meet you."

"I can't. It's not you, it's got nothing to do with you. But if you keep this up, I won't even be able to talk to you."

He was silent for a while.

"Dawn?"

"Yes."

"I—want you to undress me. And I want to undress you."

She released a breath. "Sure."

And her tension . . . now that it was just this . . . began to fade.

HE LAY IN bed, eyes closed, the cradled phone by his side.

Do you feel me in there, Dawn?

Oh yes.

Does it feel good?

It's so good, so good.

Do you know how long it's been? Ten minutes.

No . . . Too much.

Tell me it's too much for you.

Oh God, it's way too much, it's wonderful . . .

He slid off the bed. Then he went over and stood by the window.

Where was she?

If he could just meet her, talk to her in person . . . Maybe she was just afraid to say yes because someone might be on the line.

He'd come to know so many people over the years—patients, families. Some of them had to know how to find that phone, or knew someone who did; would do it for him.

There were so many Irv Goldsteins in his life, who wouldn't end up treating him the way he did.

"You saved my life, Leon."

"You were so good to my mother, Leon."

Sent him Christmas cards, would give him a gift—he never took anything expensive—sent him thank-you notes, invited him over, would call and insist.

The reporter, for instance. That private detective, what's-his-name? The bookie or gangster, whoever he was—"Whatever you want, fellow." That lawyer who knew everyone.

He'd daydreamed so many times of finding her, but never really seriously. But now it sped the blood through him to think there might be a way.

# 14

STANDING AT THE sink in the washroom, just before they were to leave, Manya said, "I feel awful about mentioning the call to you."

Lynn said, "I wish you wouldn't."

"I just want to say again, I meant it for you."

"Manya, I know. Now forget it."

Walking out of the washroom, Manya said, "I just remembered. I don't have a thing in the house to eat. Not even corn flakes. My Sam absolutely loves corn flakes."

"I hate shopping at night. I prefer early in the morning. Six. I hate those lines at night."

"Don't you? Thank God for Sam. He loves it. Problem is, you send him in for one thing he comes back with twenty. He's supposed to be back in ten minutes, it's an hour and a half. Talks to everyone."

*Sam?* Who was she kidding?

Sam, cigar centered in his mouth, was waiting as usual by the car. Manya, motioning she'd be right there, said to Lynn, "You got a second?"

"Sure."

"I just heard something and I want you to know. We're going to be going twenty-four hours in a few weeks. He's looking for more help."

"He said he might."

"Well, it's for sure. Honey," she said, "this is a gold mine. I don't understand him, should have done this a long time ago. Most of the places do. But you've got to give him credit—her too. She looks like a nitwit with that hat on all the time, but I think she's got more to say in this than she lets on. But you've got to give them credit. You ever see their ad?"

"He showed me a clipping once." Sam, she saw, was staring at the smoke as he puffed away. He seemed to be used to this kind of waiting.

"I mean in a magazine. Compared with the others. They have all these ladies on the phone with their legs *tsushprait.*"

Tsu-who? Lynn's face asked the question.

"Tsushprait. Wide open. Yiddish. Any wider they'd split in two. So in comparison his is a pretty nice, dignified ad. Phone Friend. Explore any subject, any fantasy, no limits. I'd call it—dignified. What I'm saying, I think that a lot of people we get are on a little higher level than they get."

"Then I can't picture what they get."

"I'm just saying." Manya seemed to be floundering, her face reddening. "You know, I used to work for a friend of his who had the business first. I was a friend of his wife, and they both knew I had a pretty good mouth. So he asked me would I, and I did it, and that's how I started. But let me tell you, I didn't feel as comfortable. And when he sold it to Hadley, I was even thinking of quitting. But there is a—higher level. We get more real problems."

You know, she had another Ph.D. psychologist yesterday? He said she taught him more about sex than he got out of reading a hundred books. And the day before that, an ear, nose, and throat man, a widower, who said she'd helped him get over his nervousness about having sex.

"Those other places, they're just rip-offs," she said. "Well. Anyway. I'll see you tomorrow, honey. Have a good night."

"You too. Good night."

Oh, Manya, she thought as she watched her walk to her car, don't you ever give up?

In the house, she could hear Rachel's stereo from downstairs.

122

Rachel's door was closed, but Lynn could picture her in her usual pose, sitting cross-legged on the floor in front of it, head bobbing slightly. She tapped on the door.

"Rach. Hello . . . Hello."

When the door finally opened, Rachel said, "Oh, I'm sorry. It's on loud."

"Really? No."

"It's Duran Duran," Rachel said, going back to lower it.

"I know." Oh, did she know.

Rachel came back and kissed her. Then she sat on the bed as Lynn undressed.

"What did you do today?" Lynn asked.

"Yek came over for softball." Yek was the name she and Tiffany gave a nearby day camp that they said was for princesses. "We beat them sooo bad."

"What was the score?"

"Twenty-eight to eighteen."

"How'd you do?"

"Two hits."

"Good."

They walked downstairs together. As Lynn looked in the refrigerator, Rachel said, "Mom? You think I'll be getting a period?"

"No. Never."

"*Mom.* Soon, I mean soon."

"Honey, you'll be getting it." She closed the door and looked at her.

"Not that I want it. But if you gotta have it . . . And you can get it before you get breasts?"

"Yes." They'd discussed this many times. "Absolutely. So. Let's talk about eating. We've got a lot of things here."

Instead of answering, Rachel said, hesitantly, "Mom?" Then, "You—sure you're all right? You're not worried about anything?"

Lynn, her heart suddenly beating fast, said angrily, "Rachel, why do you keep saying that?"

"I don't know. You . . . you just look worried once in a while."

"Well, I'm not. I'm not." Aware she was overreacting, she said, "I am looking for another job, you know that. So maybe if there's anything, it's that. But I'd hardly call it worried."

"Why don't you like your job?"

"I just don't like the kind of work, that's all. I'm looking for something better."

Rachel looked at her, then came over. She put her arms around her. "I'm sorry."

"Sorry? What about?"

"I got you mad."

"Oh, honey, you didn't get me mad." She felt tears spring into her eyes. "That's silly. You didn't say anything. I wasn't mad." This kid! She squeezed her hard. "I love you so much."

Rachel squeezed back. "I—got—the—best—Mom."

"I—got—the—best—daughter."

Lynn released her. "So. Let's talk about food."

"What do we have?" Rachel's voice was bright now. "Can I look?"

"Look."

Lynn watched as she peered into the refrigerator, then the food closet. Rachel was, she thought, too close to her—no new thought, but it hit her once in a while; made her wonder if Rachel wouldn't be better off if she were like so many kids at this age with their parents—moody, distant, angry, whatever. Still, she was glad she wasn't, loved it. But there could be a problem, and she would help her.

Rachel said, "What about tacos?"

"Fine. Take out the hamburger—" The phone rang, and she answered it absently. "Hello?"

Glenn said, "How are you?"

"Oh, good. You?"

Rachel waited until Lynn looked at her, then with her forefinger sketched at the air: GLEN?

Lynn nodded.

He was planning on leaving work early tomorrow, he said, maybe about eight, and he was wondering about dinner.

And as she thought about it, she saw Rachel, not even knowing what it was about, nodding yes, yes.

"YOU REALLY THINK Richie's cute?" Rachel asked Tiffany, trying to keep her on the phone. Her mother had gone out with Glenn, and she wanted to hold off facing the loneliness and night shadows of the house.

"You don't?"

"Oh, no."

"Oh, you don't know a bod. Look, I gotta go. My mom's blowing the horn."

"Seven came yesterday when the moon was up," Rachel said quickly.

"What?"

"Seven and the moon was up."

"You're goofy, I gotta go."

"Do you like Swiss almond?"

"Good *bye*."

"Chocolate mocha?"

"Goodbye, goodbye."

"French vanilla?"

"Goodbye, goodbye, goodbye." And now she was gone, and the night pressed thicker against the bedroom windows. She tried to think of who else she could call. Tracy was out, Cindy was at her cousin's . . .

This house, she could swear, sometimes creaked.

All the girls, all they ever talked about was getting raped. Don't go there, don't go here, don't do this, oh you're gonna get raped, you're gonna get raped.

She slid off the bed, fully clothed. She thought about playing her stereo, but went instead to her mother's room and turned on the TV and lay back on the bed. Her mother was really going to get mad this time. She'd been mad enough the last time when she found out Tiff hadn't come over, but this time would really do it. But if she'd told her the truth she either wouldn't have gone out or would come home, say, at ten.

She wanted her to have a good time, though she didn't know how she felt about this Glenn. He seemed nice, but she didn't know how she would feel if her mother married him. She guessed she would feel okay. Guessed so, though it was hard to really think of it.

She started thinking of her father, nice things, like taking her for the first time to the library, and the way he used to lift her up high and giggling by the elbows, things that were suddenly sad now; but she pushed him out of her mind with a press of her finger on the remote. The channels sped by. She came back to a game show.

But bor-ing.

She went to her mother's desk and sat at the typewriter. She placed her hands a little above the keys. *Dear President Reagan: Thank you for your invitation* . . .

She picked up a sheet of paper from the desk. Résumé, it said. She skimmed it, started to put it down, then read one section more carefully. Previous Employment.

She frowned. Why didn't Mom mention Master Surveys?

IT WAS A small restaurant on a narrow street, with a bay window, a little oak bar, and perhaps fifteen tables, each with a small center-piece of fresh flowers. A handsome, effeminate-looking young man led them through the hush of the place—hushed, though most of the tables were taken—and held the back of her chair, as though he'd lifted it away for her.

She looked around briefly, then smiled at Glenn—he had sug-gested this place when she mentioned that she loved duck but rarely got it as crisp as she liked. She said, "This is very nice."

"I hope you like it. My duck was very good."

The waiter appeared for drinks. Yes, Glenn said, they certainly would. "What would you like?"

"Oh, I guess a gin and tonic."

"I'll have a scotch and soda. Johnny Walker Black."

He looked at her. He was wearing a tan sport jacket, shirt open at the throat. His hair seemed somewhat fuller, longer than when she'd seen him last, and somehow it seemed even more appro-priate for his face. But his eyes, she noticed for the first time, looked a touch tired.

She said, "So, you don't know if he's really behind you?"

"No." Driving here, he'd started telling her about a meeting he'd had with the general manager—a few members of the staff had complained that since Glenn had come they had to cover too many stories a day. "Truthfully, I don't care if he is. No, strike out 'truthfully.' I do care, of course. But there's nothing I can do about it. Intend doing about it, I guess."

He really wasn't asking anyone to cover too many anythings. It was just that some of them seemed to think that a day's work was talking to a camera in front of a small fire. Maybe an exaggeration but not much. The problem was, the general manager wasn't the one who'd brought him in, the parent company did. "For all I know, he may feel in a bind—if things start turning around, it's his fault it didn't before. That's crazy, but who knows? And right now who cares? Hey, did I tell you, you've got a lovely daughter."

She smiled. "Thank you. You did, but I like hearing it again."

"So very pretty. And comes across as a real nice person."

"I'll vouch for it—she is. Sometimes I get so mad, how her father can—" She hadn't meant to talk about Jon; it just came out.

"When's the last she heard from him?"

"I'd say three months. Every few months he writes her how much he loves her, encloses some money—then no word for three months, four."

"He has to pay child support, doesn't he?"

"Oh, he's probably making next to nothing, and he's living— the last I heard, Lisbon. He had a play produced there—it had been on off-off Broadway."

"How many's he had produced?"

"I heard of three. That one, then two regional theaters."

"What about TV?"

"When we were still together he had some kind of offer for commercials, but he wouldn't touch it. I think he's very talented, but I don't know if he's the Tennessee Williams he thinks he is. Anyway, I think he's got the right lady for him now—from what I hear, a sixties child in the eighties. I do wish him well."

Their drinks came. He held out his glass and she touched it with hers. He said, "All good things."

She smiled. "All good things."

She took a sip and set down her glass. He was looking at her. He said, "You look especially pretty."

"Really?"

"Really. I don't lie. Not over important things like looks."

"Ah. Thank you."

"You're not going to say I'm pretty, too?"

"Was right on the tip of my tongue."

He smiled and handed her a menu. Everything looked so good, but she decided to stay with duck. She looked at him as he studied his. She used to have this feeling with Jon at one time, of being with someone who made you feel that people might be thinking what a nice-looking couple. She wondered what his ex-wife looked like. Undoubtedly very attractive. She was a TV reporter in San Francisco; hadn't wanted children until she could get her career going, and by then they were divorced.

He said, looking up, "I'm going to have the steak au poivre. What would you like to start with? How about crab cocktail?"

"Love it."

The duck was just to her taste, the skin crisp, and she loved the piece of steak he insisted she try. No, she said afterward, no dessert. And, no, nothing more to drink—they'd had a carafe of white wine. "I feel so good," she said.

"I'm glad. I feel terrific."

"No general manager?"

"No general manager. No Neilsen."

He reached over and squeezed her hand.

Walking out of the restaurant they were a little surprised at the heat: it had been so comfortable in there. In the car, parked around the block, cold air came from the vents moments after he started the motor. They were parked on a residential street, a little away from a street light. She felt confused all at once, a little frightened. When his hand touched her shoulder, she followed its urging and came toward him slightly, her face raised. His lips grazed her cheek—he smelled so good—then found hers. Her lips had gone rigid, almost against her will, but the gentle touch of his lips softened them. Her mouth opened slowly, her arms circled him.

He was kissing her cheeks now—almost a wisp of a kiss—then her eyes, the edges of her ears, her eyes again, then her lips. She felt the stir of him; she pressed against him without meaning to. His hands stayed on her back, her shoulders; didn't touch her

128

breasts, just held her to him. When his body eased back, hers arched forward. He kissed her mouth again, still softly; his tongue touched the tip of her tongue, kept touching it.

He leaned back and looked at her. She felt herself swallow. His eyes seemed to be asking a gentle question. She looked back at him. He released the brake. They drove quietly.

She felt her heart beating hard as he turned into the basement garage of an apartment building. As she stepped out of the car, he took her hand. They walked to the elevator. She didn't look at him as they rode up. But her skin, her whole head, felt glazed. There was a panicky tumbling inside her. It was though she were thinking for the first time, had become aware . . .

He seemed to become aware of her uneasiness as he was unlocking the door. He turned on some lights, then took her hands and kissed her on the cheek. He said, "We'll only stay a few minutes."

She looked at him gratefully.

"Would you like a drink?"

"No."

"Water? Soda?" When she shook her head, he said, "I'll tell you what." He kissed her on the cheek again. "We're going to go."

"No." The word just flew out of her—with a quick shake of her head. She wasn't dead! She hadn't let them kill her, Ed who'd never done this before, Bill up the ass, Joe let me suck . . .

"That's the most frightened no I've ever heard."

She looked at him, then put her arms around him and rested her cheek on his shoulder. He held her softly, then a little harder. His hands were rubbing her back. She felt the anxiety easing out of her. It felt so good, this. His finger touched her chin. She lifted her face. His lips touched, just barely touched, little places on her lips. Her mouth slowly opened. He seemed to have backed off a little, didn't kiss her right away. Eyes closed, she felt his face hovering just above hers, felt his breath. Then his lips rested, then pressed on hers.

He was unbuttoning her blouse. She slipped her arms out of the sleeves. He was, she sensed behind closed eyes, standing looking at her. Then his fingers were on her bra clasp, and slipping the straps free. She opened her eyes as he took her hand. She walked, her arm around him, to the bedroom.

She waited for him, eyes closed again, on the cool sheet. She heard him moving about, heard the swish and drop of clothing. The tension was coming back. She tried to think her way through it, but it swept on, heightening. And it stayed on as he kissed her, fondled her breasts, sucked her nipples, felt, squeezed, and caressed her. And entered her.

She rose with him, eased back with him, rose and fell. But she was aware of pressure on the point of her hip, the suck and slap of their bellies, the hard skin of his fingertips, and all at once she was trying to find them a field somewhere, a cabin, an empty white beach with dunes, a fireplace. And then, as she heard a sound from his throat, she arched up and released a sound from her own. But she was still trying desperately to find a place, a way.

# 15

SHE WAITED AT the doorway until Glenn pulled out of the driveway, then turned off the outside lights and double-locked the door. She checked the back door, though Rachel never forgot to lock it, and turned off all the downstairs lights but one, a habit she'd picked up from her father. Upstairs, she looked into Rachel's room, expecting to see Tiffany's form in the darkness, lying next to Rachel or on the floor in a sleeping bag. She was surprised not to see her, then angry.

She turned off the light in the hall and went to her room. She was still angry as she began to undress. Last time, Rachel had blamed it on misunderstanding something Tiffany had said. Whatever the reason this time, it was upsetting. She just didn't like leaving her alone. What was it, after two? Almost two-thirty.

She unhooked her bracelet—a thin, gold one, almost weightless—and put it in her jewelry box. She started to slip out of her skirt, but instead sat down on the bed . . . Why had she let it happen? She felt more bewildered than anything else. And running through it was a current of fear. Had she deliberately put herself to a test? She couldn't remember, didn't know. All she knew was that if she had, she'd failed.

"THAT," HER MOTHER said, "was the first half-decent breakfast you've had in weeks."

Rachel took her dishes over to the sink and rinsed them before putting them in the dishwasher. She didn't feel in her usual hurry to go out to the bus stop. She said, "You didn't tell me. Did you have a nice time?"

"When?"

"Glenn? Last night? Glenn?"

"Oh. I'm sorry. I told you where we had dinner, didn't I?"

"No. You were too mad."

"Rachel, I wasn't mad. I just don't want you to stay alone anymore." Anyway, they'd had dinner at this very nice place—it was called Andrew's.

"What did you have?"

"I had crab cocktail and—"

"Uck."

"Oh, it's good. And I had duck. Absolutely delicious. Really good. What're you going to be doing today?"

"Same as yesterday. Except horseback riding, I've got that today. And I'm going to be helping out with some of the little kids. I love little kids. Six. Five."

"I know. You always did."

"You think," Rachel said, coming back to the table, "next year I can be a CIT?" A counselor-in-training.

"If they let thirteen-year-olds."

"I don't want to be a plain old camper any more. It's for kids."

"I don't know if they let thirteen-year-olds."

Rachel watched her mother sip at her coffee. She should get going. She didn't know why she should feel uneasy about this, but she did as she said, "Mom—you know what you did?"

"What?" Her mother finished her coffee.

"On your résumé. I looked at it. You forgot to mention where you work."

Her mother set down her cup. Her face had turned scarlet. "Where did you see it?"

"In your room." She felt flustered—she'd done something wrong.

"I—did?"

132

Rachel was almost afraid to nod.

"I—*did?*" Then, "Isn't that something? It shows you what I—you know, really think of the job."

Rachel stood up. "Well—I've got to go."

"Have a wonderful day." But though her mother's face felt hot when they kissed, the hand that touched Rachel's hair was icy.

Three of the girls were at the bus stop. Did they, Tiffany said excitedly, have news. Joanne had heard from Tracy that she'd gotten a call from Mindy last night that she was going to have a nose job too, only her mother said she wasn't to tell anyone—she would just show up with it at school after Christmas or Easter break and say she'd had an accident and had to have it done.

"If it's supposed to be a secret," Tiffany said, "why did she say? And to *Tracy.*"

"Isn't that dumb?" one of the other girls said. "Tracy says Mindy just wanted her to know she was going to have one too, ha ha."

"Dumb," Tiffany said. "D-u-m-b."

The bus was coming; two boys joined them almost at the last moment, and the group piled on. She and Tiffany worked their way back to where they could share a seat. Tiffany, after plopping down, said, "Wasn't that dumb? Wasn't it?" and then leaned forward and began yelling back and forth with two girls in the seat in front of them.

Rachel stared out the window. Her hands had gone cold.

Something definitely was wrong.

Why would her mother get so upset and red over such a little thing? It was like that time she was supposed to have done a survey on some cereal box, and she forgot about it and got all flustered too. And no matter what her mother said, there were times she did look so worried. . .

"No, sweetheart, you're imagining." She must have been eight at the time, and her mother had come into her room to find her crying in bed. "No, there's nothing wrong, we're not fighting. Jon," she'd called, "Jon, will you come here?" And her Dad had sat by her bed too. He'd said, "Fighting? Oh, pumpkin. Everyone *argues.* You and I, don't we argue once in a while? No, no, sweetheart, your Mom and Dad *love* each other," and he was the one who'd stayed with her afterward.

And it had been so comforting. The quiet, angry voices she'd heard downstairs became something she'd imagined; the voices she'd heard maybe that whole year became—nothing too. They would always be going on family trips, and her Dad—well, she was maybe too old by then, but maybe not—he would still hold her up on his shoulders so she could see the bears and apes over everyone else. Forever and ever. But then the voices grew louder, sometimes right in front of her in the living room, the bedroom, the breakfast room—you never cared, who never cared, your mother, what about your father, that time when we, what about that time when you, *money,* I do miracles with money, what about a budget, your father—And he was the one who always seemed to win and her Mom to end up crying. Twice, maybe three times, she remembered running over to her Mom and holding her and screaming at him with every vein out in her throat. . . .

She kept staring out the window.

She was scared again, like she'd been scared that time when they tried to comfort her and hide things from her. Only now it was worse. All she had in the world was her Mom, and something was wrong.

A FEW MINUTES after Lynn walked into her office, Tina buzzed and said that her daughter was on the phone.

"Rach," Lynn asked quickly, "is something wrong?"

"No. My—other pair of sneakers aren't in my cubby. And I was wondering if you knew if they're home."

Lynn felt the breath go out of her. She always immediately thought the worst whenever Rachel called from camp, but Rachel always had a good reason—was going to be late, could she go to Tiffany's for dinner. But *this.*

"I don't know, how do I know? They'd be in your closet."

"I—don't remember seeing them," Rachel said weakly.

It was a lie—too out of character for her; and Lynn felt the same burst of irrational anger she had felt in the kitchen, when she'd just wanted to shake Rachel—What were you looking in my things for?

"I thought you might have seen them," Rachel said. Then, "Mom?"

134

"Yes."

"You—all right? You okay?" And now Lynn knew why she called.

"I'm fine, sweetheart. I really am." Her voice had begun to break.

"I'm sorry I bothered you."

"Don't be silly. I'm fine, sweetheart. Listen. You listen to me. I want you to have a good time today. I'm fine."

"Okay."

"So I'll see you later, okay? You just have a good time."

"Okay. I'll see you."

Lynn sat back, shaken. She stared over at the calendar on her desk. Two Tuesdays from today—that would give the Hadleys enough notice, and give her some time to save for some of next month's bills. And this was an absolute deadline. She would swear to it, on her life.

WHERE, LEON WONDERED suddenly, was he driving to? He pulled over to the curb and looked around in panic. The street, some of the houses, were vaguely familiar, but he couldn't put any of it into a specific place. All he remembered was pulling out of the hospital grounds a short while ago, wondering how he'd gotten through another day; that, and little scattered fragments as he drove—passing a Texaco station, a group of black women waiting for a bus—then suddenly this, nowhere that he knew.

He had to ask someone. He started to climb out of the car, then stopped, looking at the street sign. Heckston Street. Where did he ever hear of Heckston Street? And then with a jolt, he remembered. It was only about a five minute drive from the hospital.

He sat back, trying to clear his head, to remember how he'd gotten here. He'd been thinking of Dawn, only of Dawn—a swirl of thoughts, but the only one he could remember was her coming to his home, and he all the man he knew he could be with her.

Leon, his father had warned him the first or second night after his mother had pulled out, don't ever need a woman too much. You'll have all the women you want as long as you don't need them. And he used to say it at the craziest times, sometimes when they were half-asleep two to a bed in their little apartment over the tailor shop; sometimes in the middle of a TV show; but

135

especially the nights he'd come home from the bar, touching at things to steady himself. But then the Old Man dead in the snow on the way home from the bar, and having to move in with her and that toad of a husband with that "sister" shit.

You gotta learn how to fight back, sister. What do you do so long in the bathroom, sister? Ought to spend a few years in the service, sister. And his mother with her ah, that's just a word he uses, he wants you to be a real man. Then that look and smile when the son of a bitch heard he was going to be a nurse.

Don't ever need a woman too much. . .

And what about a woman you've never even seen?

He sat with his head back, soaked with sweat even though the air conditioner was on. After a while he put the gear in drive and released the brake. He drove, telling himself he was just going for a ride. But he kept heading in the direction of a place he knew.

Some twenty miles away, he turned onto a narrow, commercial street and drove slowly along a line of parked cars until he found a spot. He fed enough coins into the meter for two hours, then looked up the street. He couldn't see it from here—it was about a block away.

He walked slowly, past some shops, a public garage, the rear of a funeral parlor. He could see the storefront now, and its sign— Int'l Models Studio. He stopped, wondering did he really have the nerve.

He'd passed the place about a month ago, and then had called from a pay phone. For twenty-five dollars, he was told, a model would pose a half hour for him in a private room. And the "ladies accept tips."

He had come back once, but had changed his mind as soon as he'd parked.

He kept staring at the sign.

He wouldn't have to *do* anything with them, just let them pose. If it turned out that he wanted to, he could; but it wasn't that he *had* to.

He began walking quickly.

Three young women were sitting in an office off a small ante-room. They stood up when he entered, and came out. Two were in shorts, halter and high heels, and third in a miniskirt, halter and

136

high heels. They smiled, and the one in the miniskirt said, "Hello. You ever been here before?"

"No."

"No? Well, it's twenty-five dollars a half hour and—" she fluttered a hand at the other girls and herself—"you can choose whichever of us you want."

They smiled a bit fuller, and struck slight poses, as he nervously scanned them. He thought maybe the one in the middle, but she was a blonde and Dawn said she really was a blonde, and he wanted someone completely different. So, the one in the miniskirt, with the short black hair and round face and big eyes.

"That's twenty-five dollars." Then, after putting the money in the office, she led him down a little hall and into a room with a bed, two chairs, a sink and some metal hangers on the hook behind the door. She smiled after she closed the door.

"What would you like, honey?"

"Just—pose."

Why didn't he sit right here?—and after he sat down she took off her halter and put it on the bed, then unwrapped her miniskirt, and was naked. She held her breasts up and smiled at him.

"Do you like this?"

He nodded.

She pressed her belly hard and smiled. She put both hands on her pubis and smiled. She widened her legs and bent over, so her breasts hung, and she lifted her face to him and smiled.

"Do you like this?"

"Yes." He could feel the stirring.

She turned her back to him and looked over her shoulder, smiling. She stroked her buttocks, still smiling, then separated them.

"How's this?"

"Yes." It had quickened.

She bent over, still holding them. Then she stood up and put one high-heeled foot on the bed and looked at him. She made a little tossing gesture with her hair, then put that foot down and the other up.

He said quickly, "What do you charge?"

"For everything?"

"Yes." So ready.

"Oh . . ." She looked at him carefully. "Seventy-five."

He pulled out his wallet, flipped at the bills, fast—had to hurry! It was crazy, he had nothing to put on, and there was so much disease. But he didn't care, the only thing that mattered—"I only have fifty—Fifty-two. Would you take fifty-two?" Please?

She kept looking at him. Well, he looked nice. All right. She sat on the bed, smiling, then lay back as he approached. But even as he walked toward her, his heart felt suddenly in spasm, and he could feel it going.

IN THE CAR, he sat with his hands gripping the wheel, his eyes closed. His body felt frozen. It would be frozen with every woman but Dawn.

And he was going to find her.

# 16

LEON STARTED TO dial the *Journal's* number, then quickly set down the receiver. He knew what he was going to say, had even written part of it down, but his nerves were going to give him away. And you don't play around with reporters—Hillary would become suspicious.

"You're the only one I can really talk to." If Hillary hadn't said it a dozen times, he hadn't said it once. Like Irv Goldstein with his colostomy, he'd been afraid his heart attack meant the end of sex, his job, an active life; and no one else on the unit had had the patience to keep reassuring him. This past Thanksgiving, Hillary had even sent him a gift certificate for a turkey.

He dialed quickly.

*"Morning Journal."*

"I want to talk to Hillary Johns."

"Hold on."

No, he couldn't do it.

"Hillary Johns."

"Hillary?"

"Yes. Who's this?"

"This—this is Leon Owens. The hospital?"

"Leon! Hey, how good to hear from you."

No, no, it was fine calling here. No bother at all.

"Hillary. I"—he could feel his voice quivering—"I was just wondering, maybe you could tell me. I have a phone number, I'd like to find out whose it is. I thought maybe you might know."

That sounded so terrible, so awful, not the way he'd wanted to say it. But Hillary didn't ask any questions. "I imagine the only one who could tell you is the phone company. But I'm positive they won't. Unless maybe there's some legal reason—I really don't know. Did you try there?"

"No. I—was sure. It's—an old friend I'm trying to locate." And even that didn't make sense.

"No, I really couldn't tell you. Sorry. Anyway, tell me, how are you?"

For a long while, afterward, he sat by the phone, aware only of the frenzy of his desperation.

"COME ON," TIFFANY said, as the bus pulled off.

"No," Rachel said slowly, trying to think it out. "I better go home."

"Come on, no one's at my house. Come on."

Rachel looked at her. Tiffany wanted to show her some of her dumb brother's stuff, but though she was curious—more than curious—she felt really funny about it.

"You're being stupid, you know that?" Tiffany said. "You're acting real gay."

"Gay, everything's gay with you."

Tiffany put her hands on her hips. "You want to or don't you?"

Rachel kept looking at her. She did want to. She started to walk with her, slowly, a little behind her, something tugging her back. But as they neared the house, they both were walking fast.

The house had the same kind of silence hers did when she was the first one home, but now excitement, the forbidden, edged it. Tiffany's mother was supposed to be coming home from work late, her father was somewhere, her brother was somewhere—but it was as though all of them were waiting just outside.

She clambered up the stairs after Tiffany to her room. There

Tiffany, with a wide show of teeth and shoulders compressed with excitement, motioned for her to follow. Rachel looked on from the hall as she went into her brother's room, opened a closet and stood on a chair.

"He's got a secret place—he thinks," she whispered. "He's so stupid."

Rachel watched, hands clasped together at her waist, as Tiffany jumped down from the chair with a handful of magazines and closed the closet. They ran back to her room and shut the door. They sat on the floor, giggling and squirming as they started to go through them, when suddenly they whirled toward the door.

"Tiff," her mother called from downstairs. "Tiff, you home?"

"Oh, gosh." Tiffany pushed the magazines under her bed, clicked on the stereo, and flung open the door. "Mom?"

"How are you?" She was still downstairs.

"Okay."

"How did it go today?"

"Good. Rachel's here."

"Hello, Rachel."

Rachel closed her eyes. "Hello, Mrs. Bell," and immediately lowered her head. Her coming home just proved how wrong this was.

"Tiff, honey, I'm going to the market, I just stopped in for something. Want anything special?"

"No. Just—you know, those cookies?"

"Yes. Rach honey, will you have dinner with us?"

"No thanks, I have to go home."

"Sure?"

"Yes. Thank you."

"Well, I'll see you."

Tiffany waited, her mouth wide in a grimace, until the front door closed; then waited, head tilted toward the window, until they could hear the sound of her car starting in the driveway, then gradually pulling away.

Rachel said, standing, "I'm going to go home."

Tiffany stared at her. "You're something! You are!" She dropped to the floor and pulled out the magazines and opened one, rolled on her back with it, laughing, then sat up with it still open on her lap. Rachel knelt down, then sat down. They shared the same magazine.

Rachel had seen men's magazines before—kids sometimes brought them to school or camp—but nothing like this. People were really *doing* it—or almost doing it, their things just about touching, their tongues almost there; and in every combination—two men with a woman, a woman and three men, a half dozen of everyone, and there were men with just cowboy hats on, a woman with just a string of beads in her mouth—

Gross, it was really gross. How could girls grow up to pose like this?

And yet they kept looking.

"And look at this." Tiffany, who'd already seen this magazine, flipped pages toward the back. There were ads for rubber penises, and for creams for "better erections"; for "suck-off" magazines and movies of women who "loved animals"; for "part-time prostitutes," including "horny coeds"; for lists of homosex-uals and "housewives who love it"; for photos a man took of his wife, and a mother took of her daughter; for sex with a "life-sized" doll with "three holes," and for sex on the phone. Rachel had heard of recorded messages—two kids she knew claimed they'd called—but these were supposed to be for real. There was FONE FUCK ME, PLEASE, and ANN'S PUSSY'S HOT, and PEG WANTS IT BAD; there was I'M HOT, WET AND WAITING, and PHONE FUCK A STARLET, and ASS-FUCK LADIES, and I LOVE TO CUM; and there was MISTRESS EVA DOMINATES, and FETISH FEVER, and—

"Tiff, this is really weird, this one's almost like my mother's number." She turned to her with a smile.

"Where?"

Here. This one. Phone Friend. "It's almost—"

She stopped. She started to go for her wallet, for the little piece of paper, but her hand just dropped away. She didn't have to look. Dazed, a furious thumping in her chest, she quickly looked at Tiffany.

# 17

"THERE?" TIFFANY SLAPPED her temples. "She works there?"

"I didn't say that!" Rachel screamed.

"Then what're you acting so—Then what's her number, what's her number, let's see her number." She started to reach for Rachel's pocket, but Rachel jumped up. Tiffany scrambled up too. "Then let me see it, let me—"

"Shut up! Shut up!" She wanted to jump on her, claw that ugly face.

Tiffany stared at her.

"You think you're so smart," Rachel said. "You think you're a mind reader, you think you know everything!" She was only making it worse, she knew, and she began crying. "I hate you!"

"I hate you."

Rachel lashed her foot out at the magazines. Tiffany, horrified, began darting about, gathering them up. She looked up from the floor, chest pumping. "Get out of here! Your mother's nothing but a whore, a—"

Rachel ran to her, and Tiffany sprang up. They grabbed each other by the arms.

"I hate you," Rachel screamed. "I hate you, I hate you, I'll kill you!"

"I hate you!"

"I hate you!" She was crying hysterically.

"I hate you!" She was crying too.

After a while they released each other at the same time. Then Rachel ran downstairs and outside. She kept pawing at her eyes as she headed home. Hated her! Hated her! There had to be a mistake, an explanation.

But what about her mother's résumé? And forgetting about the survey?

She'd forgotten all about that.

This had to be the reason!

She stopped at the foot of the walkway to her house. She stared, then pawed at her eyes again.

Her *mother*?

No, there had to be some mistake.

"Rach?" From upstairs.

Closing the door, Rachel tried to think what to say, to do. "Me."

"Coming right down, sweetheart."

She was coming down now. In that nice blouse and shorts. Her beautiful Mom.

There was a start of tears, but her mother didn't notice as she kissed her. "How come you're late?"

"Oh, the bus. I've got to go to the bathroom." Before the tears poured. She went upstairs, closed the door and sat down on the lid. She put her teeth to her clenched hands. There had to be an answer.

After remembering to flush the toilet, she went to her room and got out the phone book. Phone Friend—it wasn't there. She looked up Master Surveys—that was listed. But why would it be the same number as Phone Friend?

There was no way she could figure this out, but maybe somehow it held the answer. Or if her Mom did work there, even if she did, maybe she was a secretary or something like that.

But she didn't know how to ask her.

And was afraid of what she'd find out.

"RACH," LYNN CALLED from the foot of the stairs. "Rach?"

She heard her door open. "Yes."

"You on the phone?"

"No."

"I was wondering. Do you want to eat out?"

"No. I'm not hungry."

"I don't mean now."

"I'm not hungry."

Lynn kept looking up the stairs. That was a queer answer for eating out later, and Rachel had apparently gone back into her room. And it wasn't like her to begin with, to go right upstairs when she came home and to stay there. Without being on the phone. Lynn kept looking, then drifted off to the kitchen and put away the dishes that were in the dishwasher.

She went back to the stairs. "Rach?" Rachel came a little farther out into the hall. Lynn said, "What should I do about food? Should I make something?"

"I'm not hungry."

"But later. You've got to have something."

"Maybe I'll get a pizza later."

Lynn kept looking. "Rach, can I see you?" Rachel came to the head of the stairs. Lynn said, "I mean, can I see you?"

"What." Rachel walked down slowly.

Lynn said, "What's the matter? Don't you feel well?"

"I feel fine."

"No, something's the matter. What is it?"

"Nothing. I'm just not hungry."

Lynn looked at her. And Rachel looked back, squarely, as though to prove nothing was the matter. Lynn said, suddenly really alarmed, "You've been crying."

"I have not."

"Rachel, I want you to tell me!"

"Oh—I had a fight."

"With who?"

"You don't know her. Some kid at camp. I've always hated her. A bitch!"

"What happened?"

"Oh—I had—I had a stupid ball, she took the ball, it was only a stupid ball, but it was mine. I hate her!"

"Well, it's hardly worth this. Is it?"

Rachel shook her head, tears brimming her eyes again.

"Come here." Lynn put her arms around her. She felt Rachel's enclose her. Then Lynn felt Rachel's arms tighten. Then they tightened around her even more.

"Mama?" It came out like a tremulous cry.

Startled, Lynn looked at her. It wasn't just the cry, it was the word—Rachel hadn't called her that in years. Rachel was looking up at her, tears pouring down her face.

"Mama"—and her hands rose, trembling, to her mouth—"what do you do?"

Oh God.

"What do you do? Do you—do you talk to—men?"

"What're you talking about?"

"I was with Tiffany—I saw—Phone Friend—Your number—" The words came out in gasps. "I'm sorry—I'm sorry—"

Oh God! She couldn't think. Help her think.

She felt her eyes filling. Her legs were threatening to sag.

"Mama, I'm sorry—"

"No, no, don't, no. Come here." For a few moments, holding her close again, she wanted to cry out yes, and I'm doing it for both of us, it's vomit, but I've been willing to work in vomit—But she couldn't say it. And now something else was forming, a way.

"Listen to me. Rach, just—just listen and try to understand."

I work for Master Surveys, she said, and I do the work I said, but they have this ugly business that I'm not part of.

"It's why I'm trying to get another job. And I will. In fact I'm going to quit tomorrow. I don't want to be there, I don't want anyone to think I've any connection with it. Do you understand?"

Instead of answering, Rachel squeezed her harder.

And kept squeezing.

SHE DIDN'T GO anywhere near Tiffany as they stood waiting for the bus. And at camp, though each bunk had to stand grouped together during the mass Pledge of Allegiance on the hill, she kept her distance. And she didn't go near her during the first swim, or in the bunk when they changed into dry clothes. But she had to tell her, and she was going to. And she did, running up to

146

her as they walked along a trail in the woods to the arts and crafts bunk.

She said quickly, "She doesn't. I know. I know for a fact. She works for a big company that has a lot of businesses, and she didn't even know about that one. And she's gonna leave. Master Surveys—you can look it up. There. I don't care what you believe. There." And she slowed up so that Tiffany could walk ahead.

But Tiffany was waiting just inside the bunk. She said, like she just wanted to get this over with, "You put away my pattern, what did you do with it?"

Rachel went to the closet she'd put it in, Tiffany following a few steps behind.

"Here."

Tiffany took it, looked at it. Then she looked at Rachel.

"You have yours?" she asked.

INSTEAD OF GOING straight up to her office, Lynn stopped at Thomas Hadley's office. He and Mary Hadley were looking in one of the file cabinets. Lynn stood in the doorway until they turned around.

"Do you have a few minutes?"

He said, "Sure," and sat down at his desk. Mary, in one of her wide-brimmers, took what seemed to be her usual position, against the windowsill.

Standing in front of his desk, she said, "I'm sorry, but I'm going to be leaving."

"Oh? I'm sorry too. I'm very sorry. May I ask why?"

"It's just time. I don't want to do this any more."

"I see. I really hate losing you." He looked at his wife, then back at her. "Look, I don't know if this will help change your mind, but maybe it will. Would you like to work out of your home instead of coming here? We get the calls, call you, and you make the calls from your home, using our number."

"I didn't know you did that."

"I don't. I don't like it. It makes me feel like I'm doing something shady. It's business, and this is my place of business. But we're going to be open twenty-four hours and I'm going to need a lot of help. And, as I say, I really don't want to lose you."

147

There was really nothing to think about. But in the few seconds she did, she thought of being home, waiting for Rachel to go to school, even mentally pushing her to school, then waiting for the first call from Tina . . . It seemed even more—obscene.

"No, I'm afraid not."

Hadley made a little helpless gesture with his hands. "Can you give us two more weeks?"

"I'd like to leave as soon as I can. I was even hoping—tomorrow."

Mary Hadley said, "I don't believe this. You're going to do this to us?"

He said gently, "Come on, Lynn, that's not fair. We don't have anyone. And we haven't done anything to deserve this."

Mary, her eyes staring out hard from under the brim, said, "Don't treat us dirty. I'm telling you don't treat us dirty."

Thomas Hadley, after a quick look at his wife, said, "Look, can we settle it this way? Two weeks at most? If we get someone, and you know we'll be trying, if we get someone tomorrow, the next day, you can leave whenever. Okay? That's reasonable, isn't it?"

But it was more the menace in Mary's words that made her agree.

# 18

THREE O'CLOCK AT last—he could get the hell out of here. And could try calling Dawn again.

"See you, Lee," Maggie said, leaving first. "And I want to see you smile more tomorrow."

He nodded. All day the fucking little cunt had been giving it to him—"Lee-on, you're just not the old Leon I knew. You don't eat with us. Don't you want to have anything to do with us now that you're a VIP?"

And all day taking care of a bunch of whining patients, when so many things were on his mind. He was so tired, so tired—he hadn't had more than an hour's sleep last night, maybe two-three hours a night all week.

He felt a spurt of adrenaline as he walked out of the unit and approached the phone booth near the lounge. But there was anxiety too—he hadn't been able to reach her all day.

"I want to talk to Dawn. It's Wing."

"I'm sorry, Mr. Wing, but she's on another line again. Would you care to hold on?"

He waited. After a while the operator said. "Hello. Who are you waiting for?"

"Dawn! I'm waiting for Dawn!"

"Oh, I'm sorry. She's still tied up. Do you still care to wait?"

He hung up.

His own phone was ringing as he walked into his house. At first he wasn't going to answer, sure it was his mother, until he remembered that two of the five people he'd called since yesterday had promised to call back if they were able to learn anything.

A young woman's voice said, "Mr. Owens, please."

"Yes."

"Would you hold a moment? Mr. Haines is returning your call."

Ira Haines was one of the people he hadn't been able to reach. Ira handled investigations for lawyers—divorces, accident cases, everything. He used to tell Leon about his cases during those weeks, last year, when he was worrying would he be able to really walk again with his new hip. I've found more missing husbands and wives, he'd said, more guys with million dollar law suits who can walk without crutches or don't need a wheelchair . . . Well, you'll be finding them again, Leon used to assure him.

"Leon, how are you?"

"Okay. How are you?"

"Fine. Good. What can I do for you?" But he misunderstood what Leon wanted. "Find an unlisted number?"

"No," Leon said, "I—have the number. Is there any way of finding out where it is?"

There was silence—the usual silence when he asked this.

"I'll—pay, of course."

"Come on," Ira said, annoyed. Then, after a pause, "I would imagine there are ways."

You see, Leon said, somebody owed him money but he couldn't reach him on the phone and he didn't know his address.

"What's his name?"

"That—won't do any good. The phone's under the name of the fellow he lives with."

"Well, what's *his* name?"

"I don't know—that's the problem."

"I'd say it is," Ira said. He paused, and Leon felt his heart plummet. Then, "What's the number?"

Leon gave it to him.

150

"Well," Ira said thoughtfully. "I know two people I can ask, but I can't promise anything. But let's see."

Leon put the phone down. He couldn't help feeling a touch of hope, but he should know better. There were so many bullshitters in this world, people who just wouldn't admit they couldn't do something.

He grabbed the phone and began dialing.

"I want to speak to Dawn. This is Wing."

"I'm sorry, she's not here. She's gone for the day." Then, "Would you like to talk to someone else?"

He hung up. He'd always known it, but hearing them say it made it worse—would he like to talk to someone else. Pass him around like a piece of shit. Talk to her or her or her or her. It's Wing, who's free?—you? you? you? They didn't care how you felt. And she, with all her beautiful talk, probably didn't care either.

And Della didn't care, and his mother didn't care—she was so damn selfish, everything was her, her—and even Freddie didn't care.

But, God knows, he had ruined it with Freddie.

He stared at the phone, wondering if Della ever told him about the award. He'd swear on anything she didn't. Before he could change his mind, he dialed his in-laws' number.

Della said, "Hello?"

He said quickly, "Please let me talk to Freddie. Just for a min—"

The phone instantly went dead. He dialed again. The phone kept ringing. He hung up and dialed again. It rang on and on. Furiously, he dialed three more times, then ran upstairs to his room and yanked open one of the two top drawers of his bureau. He realized instantly that it was the wrong one—this was where he kept his Colt, under his few clean shirts. He closed the drawer quickly, then opened the other one and took out his Nikon. He ran out to the car.

Driving to her parents' home, he didn't know why he'd even brought it. He didn't care about pictures; he wanted to see Freddie, wanted to tell him. And when he did, he'd say, "Your mother didn't tell you, did she? That's the kind of mother you got."

He'd look for him on the streets, in the playground. And if he

151

didn't find him there, he'd go right up to the house and push his way in.

He toured the neighborhood slowly, then stopped at the curb by the playground, searching out faces from the car. He tried to think what to do next. He wouldn't try to get into the house. They'd have him arrested. But for some reason he did want to just see it. And maybe Freddie would come outside. Or maybe he would be able to get a picture. He parked halfway down the street and stared at the house. It was a little after six, and there was a slight haze in the air. He could see Della's car and what seemed to be her father's car.

He wondered what they were doing in there. Having dinner? Laughing? All of them watching TV together? And the chink—there? Coming over?

How he wished he'd killed the bastard.

Yet it wasn't all the chink's fault. Hers. She'd taken everything away from him. Everything. She used to be—Dawn, his real Dawn. Leon, that was the greatest, Leon that was good, Leon you're a good person, let me hold you, Leon.

Then: Why don't you go somewhere and learn how?

Why couldn't she have stayed Dawn?

He got out of the car and stood with his arms folded hard on his chest. He could feel a momentum building inside him. It seemed to be pulling him forward.

He walked a little closer to the house. Then, after a moment, a little closer still. He stopped for almost a minute. Now, as though something had burst in him, he was striding quickly to the house. He rang the doorbell, then rang again. Still no answer. He stepped back from the door, stared at the windows.

They were in there, he knew it. They saw him, and they just weren't answering.

He pounded on the door with his fist. He rang the bell a number of times, staccatolike, then held his finger on it hard, pounding with his other fist.

He stared up at the second floor. You bitches!

He took a few steps back, still staring at the second floor. That's where they were! He stood there, breathing heavily. The bastards! If he only had his gun.

He thought of it in the drawer—the shiny metal, the grip, the

152

trigger, the bullets . . . He was going to get it. Then he'd come back and blast all of them away—Della, Freddie, her mother, father, all of them!

He whirled and ran to the car.

He made two lights just as they were about to turn red and was trying to make a third but had to stop. He kept staring up at it, urging it to turn green, then glanced in his sideview mirror. He went cold. A police car was parked about a half a car length in back, stopped for the same light. He urged himself to keep staring ahead, but something broke in him and he turned for a fast glance. And in that instant the officer's eyes caught his. Leon looked away quickly, blood gorging his face.

He stared at the light, then looked back again. And again those eyes.

That was stupid—stupid!

He kept looking at the light. The instant it turned, he pulled ahead. He wondered was the police car next to him, behind him. No, he saw, not next to him, and not in the sideview or rearview mirrors. But maybe it had drifted over to the other side. He had no mirror there, and had to look.

The police car was keeping pace there, the officer staring ahead. But the moment Leon turned to him, his eyes shifted over.

Stay the same speed, don't act suspiciously, don't slow up, don't go faster—

But all at once his car was filled with the shifting colors of the lights. The officer was waving him over.

He drew to the curb. The lights were flashing in from the rear now. The officer bent toward him at the window.

"May I see your operator's license and registration card?"

His fingers had trouble pulling them from his wallet. The officer looked at them carefully. He was tall, so tall that his revolver with its huge, grained, brown grip was within grabbing distance.

"I'll be back in a minute."

Leon watched him walk back to his car. His body went limp. He'd felt so close to grabbing it, had felt his hand going to it, wanted to yank it out, to blast away . . . He could see the officer sitting in his car.

A couple minutes later he was back.

153

"Okay. You can go. Just checking."

Leon remained there as he pulled off. He felt too drained to drive yet. He'd wanted to ask why he'd stopped him, but had been afraid to, just wanted him to go. Not that the cop, if he'd been following him, would have said.

Yet why would he be following him? Maybe Della had called the police while he was banging on the door. But if it was that, they would have arrested him. And what about that police car that had followed him to work?

The police could be just waiting, watching him. Della may have warned them. Maybe she knew what he was capable of doing. And had almost done.

# 19

"LEAVING? YOU'RE NOT," Manya said, putting down her sandwich abruptly. "When did you tell him?"

"Yesterday."

"Why didn't you tell me?"

"I am telling you. Manya, you weren't in yesterday."

"I forgot. Oh, you're not. When till?"

"Whenever he can get someone. But two weeks, tops."

"Oh damn." Then she said, "I'm being selfish. But no kidding, I'll miss you."

"We'll get together."

Manya looked at her—just a look, but it said: oh yeah. And instantly Lynn was sorry she'd said it.

"So, what will you be doing?" Manya said brightly.

"I don't know. Looking for a job."

She looked astonished. "You don't have anything to go to?"

"Not yet."

"Really? Can I ask then—why you're leaving?"

"Oh—it was horrible. Rachel found out. She and a friend got their hands on a magazine, and she saw the ad and recognized the phone number."

"Oh my God." Then with a shake of her head, "I mean it, I've always said it. I'm against stores carrying those magazines where kids can get them."

Lynn stared at her—this woman, she was absolutely unbelievable.

Manya said, "Does she know you're going to be here a couple more weeks?"

"Yes."

"Then why don't you stay until you find something?"

Lynn shook her head and let it go at that. She didn't feel up to explaining that it was going to be hard enough lying to Rachel for even two more weeks.

But Manya did stir up her worries about money. Still, there was a feeling of freedom as she walked back to the building, and even when Tina said from the console, "Wing's got the impatiencies again. Five minutes, I think three calls."

He called a few minutes later. His first words were: "I tried to reach you all day yesterday."

"Oh, I'm sorry."

"I called all day. I must have called every half hour."

"I'm sorry. I really am."

She could hear him breathing faintly during a pause. "You never think of me, do you?"

"That's not true. I've told you."

"You really do?"

"Of course." Almost all her regulars asked her this. And she'd stopped feeling the uneasiness she'd felt toward him. She watched a shadow cross the smoky glass on the upper half of her door—Mary Hadley, from the brim.

"Then why won't you see me?"

"Wing, I don't know how else to tell you"—she tried to follow the shadow, tilting her head—"the word is can't. Let's not do this any more. Please. So, tell me. Is there anything new? Tell me about the award again. You must be very happy about that."

It was a while before he said, quietly, "I don't know."

"What do you mean?"

"I just don't know." Another pause, and then, his voice even softer, "I don't—know if I even deserve it."

"Oh, that's silly, they wouldn't give it to you if you didn't deserve it. Come on, you can't really mean that."

156

"You don't know anything about me."

"Well, I know you won an award. And I know you must be a very caring person."

"You don't know anything about me."

"But I can tell. It's not hard to tell you're a good person."

"See me?"

"Please, Wing."

"See me?"

"Please. Please, Wing." She'd had insistent callers but none like this. And she made up her mind that, even though it was only for a couple more weeks, she wasn't going to take any more of his calls.

THIS TIME, WHEN he heard the phone ringing as he entered the house, he thought it might be Ira Haines or one of the others. But it was his mother. "Leon, I haven't seen you in weeks, you never call, you're never in when I call."

"I'm busy."

"Busy. Leon, I talked to Della. I talked to Freddie. Tell me the truth. Did it happen? They say you yelled at him and you left him. Tell me the truth."

"Did they tell you about the goddam chink?"

"Leon, don't yell at me. And I don't like that language."

"Tell me what you want me to say! Tell me!"

"I don't want you to yell."

"Just tell me!"

"I was talking to Freddie. He called me grandmom. *Grandmom.* Nothing's changed. He's a good boy. How could you do that?"

"Mother, will you leave me alone?"

"How could you do it? How?"

"Mother!"

"How? Tell me. I—"

He hung up, then left the receiver off the hook so she couldn't ring back. But he put it back—he might be getting other calls, though they were all bullshitters. How long was it since he'd talked to Ira? Two days? Three? And some of the others—four? Five?

He'd run out of people to ask; was down to trying to squeeze out a name or two more.

He went upstairs and dropped heavily on the bed. He was so tired, yet a racing ran through him that he felt would never let him sleep.

. . . The phone?

He didn't realize that he had fallen into a brief, exhausted sleep. His mother flashed through his mind, and he started to close his eyes again. But then he fumbled for the receiver. "Yes."

"Leon, Ira. Listen. Did I hear you right? Did you say this is listed under some fellow he lives with?"

"I—think—I'm not sure. I think that's what he said."

"Well, it was a company, not a person. Master Surveys. Got a pencil?"

HE OPENED HIS door quickly to stride out to his car, then stopped as though punched and glanced around. The police could be watching him. For a second he'd forgotten that. He saw nothing, then hurried to his car.

Delpha Avenue, he knew, was somewhere in the northeast section, but he wasn't sure where. Once he got out there, he'd ask.

He kept giving it speed, then would slow up abruptly, afraid of being stopped. His eyes kept going to the mirrors. It was almost five-thirty now, and he'd never spoken to Dawn this late; she might be gone for the day. Anyway, if there were lots of blondes, how would he even know her? And maybe she wasn't even a blonde after all.

The streets had become jammed with cars heading home from work. Horns blared sporadically. He pressed his horn. He looked at the gas—a little less than a quarter. Why hadn't he filled up?

The traffic was opening a little, and he turned at the first intersection, even though he didn't know where it led. He drove blindly, then recognized a church; that street had to be Hasted Street, which led up to the northeast. He went a little faster now.

He was beginning to see other landmarks, when the street suddenly dead-ended. U-turning frantically, he turned left at the second corner. There, straight ahead, was Walder High. And Walder was only a couple of blocks from Delpha Avenue.

He turned left on Delpha, and the addresses soon told him that he was heading in the right direction—the numbers were getting higher. He had about three miles to go.

Four more blocks. Three.

He shot a fast look at his mirrors, then looked over his shoulder. There was only a station wagon directly behind him. He started to slow up. That building, the one with the driveway leading up to it, should be it. He parked across the street. He looked at the sign near the driveway. Something-something, and Master Surveys.

There? Dawn in there?

His heart was beating so fast it almost hurt.

He got out of the car and stood staring at the building. How would he know her?

Two women were coming out of the building. He started to walk forward, stopped. Was she one of them? He couldn't even make out their faces; they disappeared into their cars too quickly. He got back in his car.

Other people were coming out, two women and a man.

He had to find a way. And he would. He didn't know how, but now that he'd found the place he was sure he'd find her. It was just a matter of time. He put his head back on the headrest, filled with a rush of almost sensuous relief.

# 20

"DID I TELL you," Rachel said at breakfast, "Tiff wants me to play doubles with her against Sunny Creek?"

"No, you didn't. I thought she plays with that what's-her-name."

"Ellen. Yeah. But she asked me."

"Are you?"

"Sure. She's good." Probably, in fact, the best tennis player in the camp.

"Oh, that's nice." More than nice. It meant that the girls were really tight again; she'd been afraid it might never happen.

"Oh, and did I give you the paper to sign?"

"What paper?"

"For the overnight Thursday. Didn't I give it to you?"

"I didn't see it."

"Oh." She started to open kitchen drawers haphazardly. "I was in here when I put it down, I'm sure I was in here."

"I'll find it. You just go."

"And I'm going to have to buy some stuff. Tiff's bringing candy. I promised cookies, chips—"

"We'll get it. Plenty of time. You just go." She held up her face for a kiss. Rachel kissed her, then waved from the door. She said, "See you."

"Have a good time."

The kids were still grouped at the bus stop when she drove by—the bus apparently was running a little late. Her immediate impulse was to tap on the horn, but they all seemed busy with one another. It was a clear morning, so sharply bright that she wished she'd brought sunglasses, yet cool enough that she didn't need the air conditioner yet. As she walked into the building she saw Mary Hadley looking her way from the rear storeroom. Mary immediately turned away; she'd barely looked at her since she'd given notice. Which was absolutely fine.

Walking into her office, she saw a large note lying on the desk near the phone.

> L. Are you free the 29th for dinner? Or lunch? Anything. On
> us. Manya Louise Tina

That would be her last day if she was here the two weeks—how nice of them. She came out of her office but Tina was too busy at the console to look at her, and Manya's and Louise's doors were closed. And her own phone was buzzing now.

Hi, Tina said, ready?

No, but go ahead.

And though she waited with the usual initial feeling of dread, there was that twenty-ninth on the note she held in her hand. It was quite a comfort. And wasn't it about time, now that she was thinking of it, that she called her friend Nan Voelmer and got together with her, really got back into the world?

AS THE BUS approached the stop, Rachel saw Tiffany maneuver herself so that she could get on first. Then when the door swung open, Tiffany jumped on and hurried down the aisle, where she plopped next to Mindy.

Rachel walked by them and sat next to a little boy of about seven, who immediately stared up at her and said, "Do you know when they pick for color war?"

"I think next week."

162

He grinned, burrowing into his shoulders in excitement, and Rachel remembered herself like that. She'd even been looking forward to it this year.

She looked up the aisle at Tiffany.

The ache growing in her was close to bringing tears. Up until yesterday afternoon, shortly before they had boarded the buses to come home, she thought she might be imagining it—that she'd caught some kids looking at her strangely and then turning away. But then she'd walked into the bunk, and there were Tiffany and a couple of girls giggling, then suddenly stopping, their faces red.

If she asked Tiffany, she'd only deny telling. But she'd probably even told her mother. Her *mother*.

And on top of everything, being so snotty. Talking to her only when she felt like it—like about that pattern; Tiffany had needed help. And then making believe she was such good friends with Mindy, when just about all she ever did was make fun of her nose.

She hated Tiffany, hated this camp.

"Tiff wants me to play doubles . . ."

And hated herself for that, though she'd done it for her mother, when the truth was that Uncle Todd, the athletic director, teamed them up.

She kept staring up the aisle. Tiffany was jumping up and down like she was two years old.

She hated this camp, though her mother, who had enough on her mind trying to find another job, must never know.

EVERY FEW MINUTES, as the end of his shift approached, Leon looked at his watch. At three, exactly, he strode to his locker, stripped off his uniform and changed into street clothes—slacks, which like all his slacks needed pressing, a short-sleeved shirt, and good but badly scuffed moccasins. He walked quickly to his car.

He started the motor immediately, but stayed parked, his hand tight on the handbrake. It was going to take all his nerve to do this, but he couldn't think of any other way. And there was the getting there. No one was following him, he'd become convinced no one was following him, but maybe they were, you could buy police. So he mustn't drive straight ahead.

He drove out of the parking lot slowly, made a right at the first intersection, then a left, a right, another left. All at once nothing was familiar any more.

He tried to think whether to turn off this street. Though he didn't know the street, he was afraid to leave it. He kept looking around as he drove. Then, slowly, something that seemed vaguely familiar was forming ahead, a building of some kind. It became a bank, then a bank he knew, and now, as though something opened in his head, he knew the intersection and where that street led to.

Twenty minutes later he was sitting staring at the building from his car. His eyes went to the sign again: Thomas Hadley, CPA, and underneath: Master Surveys, Inc. That, as he'd been thinking half the night, didn't make sense. A CPA and some kind of survey company, whatever that was. What could they have to do with Dawn?

Maybe it was all wrong, maybe whoever had gotten it for Ira had gotten it wrong.

He felt the pull to go in there, look around, ask.

In that plain, ugly building, Dawn? *There?*

A woman was walking out the door. He grabbed the door handle to twist it open, but froze. He knew what he wanted to say, he'd gone over it so many times—"Hello, I'm Wing," and she'd be maybe angry or shocked, and he'd plead, "Wait, let me talk to you." That is, if he did want to talk to her—she might be so ugly he might not want to. But if he did want to, he'd say something that would make her know it was at least safe to talk to him, out here near the building with the sun still out. She'd know it too, from his face.

The first woman had entered her car; he watched, still trying to decide what to do, as she pulled out of the parking lot. A few minutes later two others came out. He drew in a bladelike breath, held it. Then he slid out of the car and walked quickly to the driveway.

"Pardon me."

They looked at him. One tilted her head questioningly.

He said, "Do you know if there's a laundromat around here?"

164

"No, I'm afraid I don't," and the other shook her head. But he asked her anyway. "Would you happen to know?"

"No, I don't."

He went back to his car. It was hard to really tell from those few words, it was maddening, but he didn't catch that voice. He wondered could she be the one he'd missed, and if there were any more in there, and how many.

Couldn't do this too long at one time. Sure to arouse suspicion. And couldn't approach too many at the same time; only one or two would say anything, and then you could never approach the others.

He'd wait for one or two more. Then if he had to, he'd come back.

# 21

LYNN GLANCED AT her watch as she walked quickly from her car to the building. She'd used another of her lunch hours to go out on an interview: salesperson at a small boutique. Although she admitted having no experience selling, the woman seemed to like her and had left her with the feeling she might get it. But, again, it wouldn't come even close to paying the way, and she'd have to look for a second job, evenings.

Manya was just coming out of the washroom. She stopped to talk, motioning to Tina, who was gesturing that she had a call, to hold off, just hold off.

"Honey, I've just had the most—what would you call it, rewarding experience. I've had a lot of them, so many, but I can't remember any like this. Maybe there were, but this . . . A *doctor.* You'd think, a doctor. Very, very big man. *Rich.* Tells me he has horses, the whole thing. But he tells me he's depressed—no, no, he doesn't come right out and tell me, but I can tell he's sort of rambling, and I tell him, I say you sound very down. And it just came right out.

"*Down*—he wants to commit suicide. You know, a lot of people tell you, they use the word, but I know enough psychology—I've learned enough psychology here—I know enough he really means it. He's been to psychiatrists, psychologists, everything, but he's depressed. Why?" She kept gesturing, annoyed, at Tina. "He's got nothing going with his wife, he has a ladyfriend he likes but—he, you know, he can't, he just can't function. Anyway, I talked to him. You know what he feels guilty about? His children. He's with the lady but he's thinking what would my children think. So we talk, he talks, I talk. Beautiful. I should be a psychiatrist, he says. Better than any psychiatrist. Honey," she said, walking to her door, "I'm telling you, I feel so good."

Lynn looked at her until she closed the door. It was hard to tell when Manya was exaggerating. If it hadn't been for Louise, she wouldn't even be aware it ever happened. But one thing sure—no one was better suited for this.

Tina buzzed as soon as Lynn closed the door. She said, "I meant to ask. Did you do anything to your hair?"

"No."

"It looks a little different. Nice. Ready?"

"No, but whenever."

"I know what you mean . . . It's your truck driver. He's calling from Albuquerque."

Settling back, she reflected briefly on the interview. If she got it, she'd definitely need another job . . .

Frank said, "Dawn, how's it going?"

"Good. How are you?"

"Still rolling. I'm in Albuquerque—just dropped off a load of furniture. Ever been here?"

"No, not there either. I'm afraid I haven't been to a lot of places."

"Just hop in the cab, hon."

"I wish."

He laughed. "I think my old lady's finally going to be riding with me. I don't know if I told you—the kids are gone. So we've been talking about it off and on. She might do it the last year before I give it up. Maybe this year. I don't know. All's I know it's a tough life, a grind. A hard buck. I'm thinking more and more of that farm."

"You said you think in a few years."

"Yeah, three. But I don't know. The rig'll be paid off, but I don't know, I told you my sister-in-law's sister owns the place. She and her husband. And they promised when they sell, they'll sell to me. But I don't know, I hear they're thinking of selling now. And no way I can do it."

"Did you ask them?"

"No, I'm sorta afraid of the answer."

"I think I'd ask. You might be worried over nothing."

"You may be right."

"And if they are, I'm sure you'll find another place. I know they're just words—"

"No, you're right. But I've had my eye on this place. Well, we'll see. So. How are you?"

"Good."

"Reason I asked again—it's none of my business—but you— you know, sound a little low."

"No, I'm fine."

"If you are, just say it."

"No, I'm fine." But she felt impelled to tell him she was leaving—she'd developed a feeling of friendliness toward this truck driver, whose description she didn't know, who kept calling her from different parts of the country. "I want you to know I'll be leaving here in a few days."

"Aw no. Aw no." With a trace of hope: "You going with another place?"

"No."

"Just had it, huh?"

"Let's just say it's time I did something else."

"I'm going to miss you—I really am . . . Hm," he said, as though it were just hitting him. "Before we hang up, will you do me a favor?" He seemed hesitant. "Is there—look, you know—is there someone there you'd recommend?"

"THIS," MANYA SAID, standing up from her desk to leave with Lynn, "has been an unbelievable day. First the doctor. Then I had a young fellow, he was going to leave his wife, I can swear I saved that. And then just before, ten minutes ago, I had this old man, he said he was seventy-four—"

"Manya," Tina said at the doorway, "your phone's off the hook."

"Oh."

"Could you take one more? He's asking for you."

Lynn started to leave the office, but Manya motioned for her to stay. "I want to talk to you." She picked up the phone without sitting down.

"Yes, doll . . . Oh, sure . . . So how've you been? . . . That's good, love, that's real good . . . Sure . . . Sure. Of course I remember . . . No. I wouldn't let you come alone. Would I let you come alone? I swore, and I mean it . . . No, I've told you, I've been honest. I don't do that for everyone. I tell them I do, but . . . Yes, sweetheart. Yes. Let me get more comfortable here, let me get this thing off."

Lynn closed the door quietly behind her. Tina's replacement was at the console, hers was in her office, and Manya's was reading a paperback, ready to go in. She'd known this all along, yet it still came with a touch of surprise—that she'd never heard any of the girls actually talking before; maybe, at most, wisps of a word or two if a door wasn't completely closed. She'd felt very uncomfortable in there, as she'd always assumed she would. There was even a little feeling, which lingered, of hearing herself talk for the first time.

Manya, in her flowered blouse and chartreuse slacks, came out in two or three minutes. "I'm sorry I held you up, hon. But I've been so excited." She sat down to adjust her shoe. The old man? she said. The one she'd been telling her about? Has no one in the world, no one, and he was ashamed he called, was embarrassed. His wife was dead, she said, standing up, his children were God knows where, he was living alone, was afraid he'd have to go into a nursing home.

"He's got someone to call now," she said, as they walked down the stairs, "someone to talk to, someone—you know. I told him he should go out, meet women, he says I'm right, he will. It really makes me feel good."

They walked outside, but Sam wasn't there yet—she remembered he had to pick up the car at a garage. When Lynn said she'd wait with her, Manya, said, "No, that's all right, you go."

"No, I'll wait. He might run into a problem."

170

They stood just inside the doorway, in the air conditioning. Manya kept looking out the window. She said, "People are such hypocrites. They look at this, they think—sleazy, this, that. Sure, there's sleaze in it. God. But you tell me anything that doesn't have sleaze. Business? Look, the medical profession? Lawyers? Accountants? The police? Hypocrites, really. They should just spend a day like I did today, like I've done day after day—"

Lynn looked at her as she looked out the window again. This, the stories—Manya, she sensed, was disturbed by her leaving.

"Did you ever get a call from a homosexual?" Manya said, still looking out.

"Not that I know."

"I can't count how many. They wanted to be men. I think everyone of them said I helped them. That's a good feeling. Priests, I had two priests. Ministers. I had an orthodox Jew. I must have had a thousand, I don't know, but he said he was an orthodox Jew." She smiled for the first time, and turned. "He wanted to know was I Jewish. I said are you proposing? Are you taking me home?"

Lynn laughed. "Was he?"

"No, he just wanted to know was he with a Jewish girl . . . I'm trying to think who else, there've been so many. Oh, a policeman. A *sergeant*. One of the homosexuals. That's trust, someone like that tells you something like that. Put himself right in my hands. I wouldn't do that with a psychiatrist . . . Ah," she said after a moment, "Sam."

His car was turning off the driveway. "I really pinned your ear," Manya said. "But I feel so good I wanted to share it." They stepped outside. She said, as though she had to say something else, "You going to have dinner at home?"

"I'm sure."

Sam, his lips pursed around his cigar, stepped out, gave both of them a quick glance, then took his dogged little walk around the car to open her door. Manya trailed after him. She said, "Thanks."

"Take it easy. Have a good night."

They pulled off as Lynn walked toward her car. The sun bounced off the hood. She felt around in her handbag for her key. She tried to unlock the door, but had the key upside down.

"Miss?"

A man was standing on the sidewalk, partly on the grass of the incline to the parking lot.

"Can you tell me what time it is?"

She looked at her watch. "It's almost half-past five."

"I'm sorry, I didn't hear you."

"It's half-past five."

She inserted the key in the lock. She turned it.

"Dawn."

She went rigid, icy. And then, without thinking, whirled around.

# 22

HER HAND DARTED for the door handle, but he took a step up the incline and she knew in a blurry instant that there was no way she could get in the car before he reached her. She said, "Wait," and extended her arm in warning. "Don't come closer."

"Don't run. I'm not going to hurt you."

"I won't, but just stay there." God, where were people? A few cars sped by, but what would he do if she tried to run out to the street?

"Promise you won't run."

"I promise. But don't come closer." His eyes, as he stared up, were huge, absolutely wild.

"I just want to—talk. Just talk."

The voice—she was sure it was Wing. Be smart, be clever. "Well then, let's talk."

"Not like this. Not from down here. Don't be afraid of me."

"Well, you scared me. I didn't expect it. I'm really shaking."

"No, don't."

"You can understand that, can't you? I'm nervous."

"Don't be."

He took another step toward her.

"Stay back."

"I'm sorry." He took a step back. "But I want to talk to you."

"I want to talk to you. But I'm still shaking." She held out her hand. "Look."

"I'm sorry. I didn't know how else to do it. I didn't know how. And I need you. I—I didn't even know how—beautiful you are. You are, you're beautiful . . . Listen to me. I—I've got money, I've got over twelve thousand dollars. Fifteen, almost fifteen thousand dollars. I was going to buy a car. I've never had a new car. But I'll buy you something. Just—see me, just be friends."

"You wouldn't have to buy me anything." Where were people? *Someone?* "That's so kind of you, but you wouldn't have to do that."

"Just—be close . . . Dawn, talk to me."

"You wouldn't have to give me anything," she said.

"I want to."

"But you wouldn't have to." And all at once she grabbed the handle and twisted it.

Somehow she was in the car, slamming the door shut with one hand, seeking out the ignition with the other. With the first roar of the motor she shot back out of the parking spot, then forward, turning into the driveway, past him, then onto the street even though cars were coming fast. With frantic glances into the mirrors she wove past cars, forcing her way over to the right lane to get off this street, to make a turn at the first corner. She made the turn, then another, went straight, then through the thunder of her heart sought out the street that would take her to the street that would take her home.

A nightmare, she was in a nightmare!

She only wanted to go home.

But if he knew where she worked, maybe he knew where she lived!

Lynn pulled into the driveway, started to climb out, then stopped, telling herself she had to act calm, look calm, mustn't scare Rachel.

She dropped her keys at the door, had trouble picking them up. Inside, she stood for a moment with her back to the door, breathing through her mouth, heart pounding up through her head.

"Mom?" From Rachel's bedroom.

"Yes." She could barely get it out.

"Hi."

"Hi."

"I'm on the phone."

She had to make a call too. Fast. But which phone? Where wouldn't Rachel hear? Down here? She decided on up there—Rachel might come downstairs in the middle. Upstairs, in the hall, she called to Rachel's open door, "I'll be on the phone," and closed the door to her room and went to her desk. She reached for the phone, then remembered that she didn't know Thomas Hadley's office number. She flipped through the phone book rapidly, pausing once to glance at her watch. Five after six. Please let him still be there.

She dialed quickly. Mary Hadley answered.

"Mary. Lynn." Her voice was low, trembling. "Mary, was anyone just in asking for me?"

"Not that I know." She asked her husband, then, "No."

"Let me talk to Mr. Hadley."

He said, "Yes, Lynn."

"Mr. Hadley—when I was leaving—a man—a man called me Dawn."

"Who? Where?"

"Outside. As I was leaving. Someone who's been calling."

He still didn't seem to understand. "Someone you know?"

"Mr. Hadley"—her voice was a fierce whisper—"someone called me *Dawn*. A man."

"But it has to be someone you know."

"No—one—knows."

"But it has to be. I mean, how would he know?"

"I don't know, that's it, I don't know."

"You must have told someone. How would he know you? I—mean, you must have told *someone*, a friend. . . . Are you even sure he really said Dawn?"

Lynn closed her eyes.

"Lynn?"

"Goodbye, Mr. Hadley."

She put down the receiver slowly. She squeezed her hands tightly on her lap. Police? *Police?* She couldn't tell the police without risking its getting back to Rachel. And even if she could tell them, which she wouldn't, ever, what good? He—Wing—it had to be him—hadn't done anything to her. Hadn't even threatened her.

"Mom? You still on the phone?"

"No."

"Would you help me with this thing?"

Rachel was trying to hook on a little bracelet. Lynn did it for her, in the hall. Rachel said, "That Tracy."

"What's the matter?"

Oh, it was Tracy's sister's birthday, and she was having these little kids over, and last week Tracy asked if she'd sleep over too, because she wanted company, she couldn't *bear* it alone. "I don't want to *go.*"

"Then don't." In fact she didn't want her to, didn't want to be alone.

"But she says I promised."

"Well—tell her you're taking it back. I don't know. Whatever you want to do."

"I just told her. She's mad."

Rachel's phone was ringing again. While she went to answer it, Lynn went back to her desk. She squeezed her neck. What should she do? Run—but where? And for how long? Wherever she went with Rachel, they'd have to come back.

"Mom"—she was in the doorway—"I don't know what to do. She's mad."

Lynn looked at her. No, Rachel mustn't be here tonight! At least not tonight!

She said, "Why don't you go?"

Rachel grimaced. "A bunch of little kids."

"But you have fun with Tracy. Why don't you?"

"I don't know."

"Go, I want you to."

"She's—mad."

176

"Rach, go, you'll have a good time."

"You're—all right?"

"Of course I'm all *right*. What kind of talk is that?"

Rachel kept looking at her. Then she turned and went back to the phone.

Lynn stared at the doorway. She mustn't let her walk over there alone.

STANDING AT THE kitchen phone, she dialed Glenn's number quickly, before she could change her mind.

It was almost with relief that she heard it keep ringing. Still, she let it ring on.

He was probably still at the station—eight was still early for him. She set the receiver back on the hook, wondering should she try him there. No. It had been hard enough calling him at his apartment.

But she was so nervous.

No, she was terrified.

She couldn't get comfortable in any room—not the living room, her bedroom, the kitchen. But the kitchen seemed the brightest in the night.

She wondered again should she call Nan Voelmer, invite herself over. But again no. She mustn't leave the house—she'd never be able to bring herself to walk back in tonight. She had to stay, wait, see, just as she couldn't run away with Rachel, knowing she only had to come back, that running hadn't ended anything. And this thought she had far back in her mind that maybe she would confide in Nan, was crazy, she would never do it. Nan, with her picture perfect life, could never understand.

But she just couldn't sit here either, alarmed by every glimmer of a headlight beam that passed across a curtain, every sound from outside. And even by silence. Especially, it seemed, by silence.

She went to the cabinet where she kept the phone books. She brought one back to the table, went through it quickly, then began dialing before she might jumble the number.

A man's voice answered. It gave the impression of women operators gone, and a building emptied out. "Channel Five."

"I want to talk to Mr. Norlund."

177

"Hold on. I'm not sure if he's left." After about a minute another man came on. "Mr. Norlund's phone."

"Is he there?"

"He's out in the newsroom. Can I tell him who's calling?"

Suddenly she wanted to hang up. But it came out. "Tell him Lynn Shephard."

Glenn was on in a few moments. "Hey, how nice to hear from you. How are you?"

"This is dreadful, isn't it? I tried to reach you at home—"

"Dreadful? This is the first good news all day. Hey, it's good to hear you."

"I'm going to talk real fast. If you've got nothing to do and would like to stop over afterward—"

"Love it. But it wouldn't be till maybe ten. Maybe after the eleven news, I don't know."

"Whenever. I'll make some supper."

"No, no. No trouble. I've eaten. Coffee, that's all. I just want to see you."

"Come over whenever you can."

"As soon as I can get out of here."

She immediately began looking in the refrigerator and cabinet for what she might give him if he changed his mind. She had cold turkey, could make club sandwiches. She had fettuccine, she could make fettuccine Alfredo. Or chili, she had chili, but did she have any more chips?

It was only when she'd stopped busying herself and had closed the cabinet door that she became aware of her heart's quick beating, of all the things she'd managed not to think of for a while.

She sank down slowly at the kitchen table. She needed help, someone she could share this with, trust.

She wondered could she tell him.

OCCASIONALLY SHE WOULD look at him as they sat on the sofa, watching the Channel 5 newscast. It was impossible to tell from his expression what he thought of it. His eyes stayed slightly narrowed, his face impassive, whether he was sitting back or leaning forward or taking a sip of black coffee. If anything, she felt he was displeased about something. So she was surprised when

178

he said during a commercial that he thought the co-anchors were the best in the city—people would find out for themselves if they'd just tune in. Afterward he seemed pleased and excused himself to make a call to the station.

When he came back, she said, "Are you sure you don't want anything to eat?"

"No. Nothing."

"More coffee?"

"That I'll have. I'll get it."

"No, stay there."

But he followed her into the kitchen. He sipped at it, standing against the counter.

She said, "How's it going with your boss?"

Oh, he said as they walked back together, things seemed to be going smoothly of late, and there didn't seem to be any more staff revolutions on the horizon. In fact, he was quite pleased at how well the new people he'd brought in and the veterans were working together.

He set down his cup and took her hands as they stood by the sofa. He said, "How're you doing?"

"Okay." And in that instant she knew she couldn't tell him.

He touched at the hair on her forehead. He kept looking at her. Then, slowly, he brought her to him, held her with his cheek against her hair. Her arms rose around him. She just wanted to be like this, just like this, just be close. She was so scared.

She felt her lips begin to tremble.

Why couldn't she tell him?

He sat down with her, his arm across her shoulder, his cheek still on her hair.

So scared. So scared.

He was touching her cheek, stroking it. He kissed her forehead lightly, then just held her again. She wished she could just fall asleep this way.

He said softly, "Hey, you down there."

She closed her eyes. She loved the feel of the rise and fall of his chest. His hand was rubbing her shoulder, occasionally squeezing it. Now he was squeezing it harder. He lifted her face and looked at her. His lips touched her lips, just touched them, and then he

179

looked at her again. He kissed the tip of her nose. Now his lips were on her forehead, then went to her cheek, then to just under her ear, stayed there, touched her ear. She kept turning her face with his lips. They were on her throat now, then her lips. She opened her mouth with his, felt his tongue, drew it in.

He was unbuttoning her blouse now, and she arched her body to help him unsnap her bra. It slipped off like a breath. She felt so free without it, but wanted him close again. She held his head to her breast as he sucked at the fullness, then lingered on the nipple; she quivered and held him tighter, then held him as he sought out the other breast. Her shoulders were in spasm; she clutched him harder, then raised herself to help him undress her. She waited for him, head thrown back, then opened her mouth to his lips again, and with a sudden gasp circled him. She tried to keep him to her, kept meeting him, meeting him, then rose higher against him, longer, then rose, finally, to the highest arch, tried higher, sought higher, then fell back with a little cry, holding him, feeling the subsiding, not wanting it to go, never to go, never.

But it was going, and though he held onto her, was kissing her, was touching her face, her hair, the fear was seeping back.

# 23

HE SAT IN the kitchen, in the light of the neon fixture, then stood up and walked back into the living room and sat down on the sofa. But almost immediately he wanted to stand up again, to sit somewhere else, to pace.

If he could only stop the fury in his head. But that bitch, that fucking no good bitch! To do that to him, to talk to him so—nice, to say yes I'd like to talk, to even smile—and then *that*.

He sat leaning forward, his hands clenched between his knees. He kept tightening them.

But why, with all this hate, did he still ache for her?

She'd even lied about such a little thing, her hair, about being a blonde. So why this ache?

The phone rang, but he didn't want to go to it. But as it threatened to ring itself out he suddenly wanted to hear a voice— someone's, anyone's, even his mother's.

"Yes."

"Leon. Me." Della—each word angry. "Now you listen to me. You're the one beat up Dr. Wang, aren't you?"

He felt something heavy drop in his chest.

"Aren't you? Aren't you?" When he didn't answer she said, "You listen to me! Now you just listen to me! He was here, we were all here, you came banging on the door like a crazy—He saw you drive away. And he's sure it's the same car he saw drive away when he was beaten up! You hear me? You hear me?"

"I don't know what—"

"You're a liar, a goddam liar! Now you hear me—"

"Why didn't you answer?"

"Because you're crazy, you're insane. Now you hear me. You ever come here again, you're in jail. And you ever come near him again, he won't call the police, he'll kill you. You hear?"

"Why didn't you answer? All I wanted was to tell Freddie—"

"Freddie! You son of a bitch, you can forget Freddie! Not in a million years will you see him! You hear me? You hear me?"

And she hung up.

He sagged onto a chair.

He sat in the silence, staring at the floor. Then he lowered his forehead to his hands. He kept squeezing, hard. In all the hate and aching in him, he couldn't tell whom he hated and ached for the most.

HE LEFT THE nursing station precisely at nine and went to the phone booth. He had first started calling from home, in the half-light of morning, then every half hour from here. Now, for the first time, someone answered.

"I want to talk to Dawn."

"I'm sorry, she's no longer with us."

"She won't be in?"

"I just said she's no longer with us. Would you like to talk to someone else?"

He put down the receiver. He'd been afraid of this, sure of it; and now he could never tell her—"I'm sorry I scared you, it was my fault just showing up like that, I don't blame you."

It would be a lie, but he would say it. Just to have that voice again—that voice with that beautiful face. But she shouldn't have run. She'd seen his hands—they were empty. And he'd pleaded with her—just talk to me, I won't come any closer.

She shouldn't have run. Not after all the times they'd talked. All those things she'd said.

182

Someone, as he began to walk back to the unit, said in passing, "Lee?"

Had he nodded back? He'd tried so hard to nod.

Using him all this time. Making fun of him. And yet why the ache? Why wouldn't it stop?

Maggie, standing outside 316, called to him. The aides had disappeared, would he help her get Mrs. Fineman back in bed? He helped lift her, close to two hundred and fifty pounds of her, from a chair, and guided her, wobbling, over to the bed; helped hoist and turn her.

"Thanks, Lee."

They still couldn't tell? That his skin barely held him? That everything inside him was jumping and twisting and beating; was on fire?

"I'll check Mellon's IV." His own voice, somehow. And now doing it when he didn't care if Mellon let out a scream and died, if Fineman died in her blubber, if 318 pulled out her tubes, if 319 punched through her incision.

"Lee, it's for you."

Maggie held up the phone as he started to walk by the nursing station. He took it from her. "Yes."

"Lee. Hal Klein."

"Who?"

"Hal Klein. Public relations." They were preparing a press release on the three nominees for Nurse of the Year, hoping to get newspaper and TV coverage on the nominations as well as on the awards dinner next month. "I'd like to set up a time to get your picture taken. Could we possibly do it today?"

His picture? His *picture?* "I can't today."

"What about tomorrow?"

No, tomorrow wouldn't be good either. He just couldn't.

"It really won't take very long. How about the day after? We really can't wait longer than that."

All right, he heard himself say.

He sat down numbly. His legs had gone weak. And something—it felt like a vein, a lot of veins—seemed to be ballooning in his forehead.

She'd seen his face. She mustn't find out who he was.

But where was she? What could he do?

LYNN WOKE WITH a sense of having slept well, then with the sudden feeling that she was late. But as she flung away the sheet and swung her legs off the bed, she remembered that it didn't matter, that there was no job to go to. And, with this, the hot beating in her chest was back, everything was back.

It was Wing, wasn't it?

Love me, tell me you love me!

Then: Hold me, just hold me.

How had it begun? She couldn't remember him from the beginning. Just another voice, she had trouble separating the voices. She could even be wrong, it might not be Wing. But which other one could it be in that whirl of voices that asked her to say what? Had wanted something where?

And her—had that really been her?

Although she was there just yesterday, it was hard to believe she'd ever been in that world.

LEON SAT FULLY clothed in bed, the phone next to his outstretched legs. Every so often he would look at his watch. Then, though only ten minutes had gone by since the last time he called, he dialed Master Surveys's number. At the first sound of a voice, he quietly hung up.

It was after midnight. He'd been doing this since ten.

They had to close some time, didn't they? After all, he'd kept calling them early this morning and no one answered until nine. So, they had to have left some time last night.

Unless this morning was a fluke. Unless someone there was out sick or something.

He started to dial again, but it was too soon, they would get suspicious. He stood up, wondering what he'd do if they never did close. Unable to hold off, he came back to the phone. But someone still answered.

He would give it twenty minutes now. Fifteen. He would give it fifteen minutes. But less than ten minutes later he dialed again. And this time it kept ringing.

The phone still to his ear, he eased himself onto the side of the bed. He kept listening, waiting for someone to pick it up. Then he looked at his watch.

They'd left sometime between two and ten after.

He sat with his hands clenched against his mouth. Could he do it? And why was he even doing it? Even if he did learn where she lived, what then?

He just had to know.

He stood up quickly, wondering should he go now. He wouldn't get there until maybe three. That would be all right, but if he waited until tomorrow he could be there earlier.

So even though everything inside him was racing to go, it was best to wait.

But as he lay in bed trying to sleep, as three o'clock passed and then four, the thing that scared him was that he'd missed his chance, wouldn't have it again. That feeling stayed with him all day, and by eleven o'clock that night, though he knew it was much too early, he was ready to leave. He stood in the foyer, trying to remember one by one what he'd put in the car. A flashlight, a screwdriver, pliers, a wrench—

He stopped.

Had he decided not to take it? Or hadn't he thought of it? He wouldn't go out in that night, wouldn't go there, without it. Quickly he walked upstairs and went to the bureau drawer and took out the Colt. It felt reassuring in his hand.

A couple hours later, as he stared at the dark building from his car, he wondered again if he had the nerve. He decided that if he did go he'd go light; would take only the flashlight and screwdriver and the pliers. And the gun, of course. He put them in various pockets and looked at the building.

Her name and address had to be there.

He sat staring, unaware he was rubbing his thighs. Was it better to walk across the street or drive up the driveway and park on the lot? He decided it was better to stay parked here, with this scattering of cars along the curb, than to be the only car up there.

He looked to his left, then to the right, and then with a quick movement opened the door and closed it quietly behind him. He walked swiftly across the street, up to the driveway, and through the darkness to the rear. Where could he get in? There had to be a back door, a side door; he didn't want the front. But there was no door, no—Yes, here. But it was a solid door, had no glass. He tried a few of the windows in the rear. Locked.

Shielding the beam with his hand, he clicked on the flashlight and peered into a window. A plain little lock. He began tapping the back of the flashlight against the glass at the lock. It refused to break. He took out the revolver and struck the glass with the butt. Pieces scattered. He ran, hunched over, to the bushes edging the grounds, crouched near them. If anyone heard, or there was a burglar alarm . . .

He gave it maybe five minutes, started forward, then gave it several minutes more. He reached through the opening, turned the latch. The window opened easily.

He climbed in, closed the window and shot the beam around, low. Where could he even begin to look?

He seemed to be in a storage room of some kind—there were a lot of cartons, cleaning supplies. He walked down the corridor. Near the front was a large office. He grabbed a handful of papers from the desk, held them low so he could look at them, then threw them away. A Rolodex—he spun it quickly. A million names. He opened the doors of the desk—stationery, ledgers of all kinds, a checkbook, a box of candy bars.

He put the checkbook on the floor, looked at the stubs under the light. Scribbled names of companies, it seemed. And other names he couldn't begin to make out. He flung the checkbook against a wall.

He opened several drawers of a filing cabinet. A million papers. He grabbed them up, glanced at them, scattered them. He could make out a staircase in the hall. He walked up. It led to a large room, what seemed to be a reception room, with offices all around. He went to the reception desk, looked at the Rolodex, went through the drawers, scattering papers, books, as he looked at them under the flashlight. The offices now—their papers, cards, drawers, scanning them swiftly, throwing them aside. Suddenly he stopped. The beam had caught a couple of words on a card; now he held the card closer to it.

You really turn me on, you know that? I didn't think anyone could anymore. (DENY IT IF HE SAYS YOU'RE FAKING.

SUGGESTION:) Honey, (SAY IT SLOW) you don't have to believe this, but I'm telling you. I'm getting real wet. I'm doing it and I'm getting all wet. Are you real hard yet? Tell me when you're ready. I didn't think this could happen to me. (IMPROVISE UNTIL HE GETS IT OFF)

He grabbed another in the pack.

If I were there I'd climb on it. (IF HE WANTS THIS, SAY SOMETHING LIKE:) Hold it while I climb on it. Are you holding it? Let me slide down on it—slow—and—easy. Do you see my big tits? Can you see them? They're bouncing up and down. (IMPROVISE)

He flung away the cards. He stood with his hands on the desk, head down, his weight on his arms. His arms began to tremble.

Even —this? Not even her own—words?

He felt a sudden swirling in his head, had to sit down. He felt cold, clammy; his heart was knocking.

And he'd let her drive him crazy. Crazy. Had become a madman.

A madman. Had even come close, this close, to killing Della and Freddie. Della and *Freddie! Freddie!* And touching that little girl. . .

He stood up. He looked around wildly. This fucking whore bitch! He'd still had a family—his Della, his Freddie. No wonder Della said you're crazy—she'd driven him crazy.

Filth.

He swept everything off the desk, began tearing through the drawers again. Where did she live? Who was she? It had to be here somewhere. Where?

He went to the one office he hadn't been in yet, but nothing there either. Yet one of them had to be her phone, her desk. Which? He started to search the others again, but sank exhausted onto a chair.

He glanced at his watch—going on six. Had to get out of here. But how could he just leave? He wanted to put bullets in the walls, the chairs. Instead he took out his screwdriver and ran it along

187

the walls. He stabbed it into chair after chair, grabbed the handle and pulled and ripped. Punched it into pictures.

He headed downstairs, the flashlight off because it might be seen from the street. He looked in the large office again. The main whore place, it had to be! He raked the desk, the walls, the sides of the cabinets. Then, though drained, he began searching through the papers he'd thrown to the floor, went through the remnants of the files again, then the desk drawers. He glanced through a large ledger he'd already looked at—it was filled with columns of numbers. He threw it away. He lifted another.

He paused and looked at it closely. It was labeled Payroll.

He'd already gone through it, he was sure, but he sat down with it on the floor, his back against the desk. There were about fifteen names listed, with addresses, phone numbers, and what apparently were social security numbers—most of them women, maybe all of them women. Three, he noticed, had check marks next to them, along with "Term." and a date.

One of the dates, he saw, was the day before yesterday.

He looked at the name. Lynn Shephard.

Yes. He felt his excitement growing. Yes. Terminated the day before yesterday.

# 24

THE BUSES AND counselors' cars filed slowly through the camp's twin totem pole entrance and along the gravel path to the large parking lot. The children scrambled out, yelling and dashing about, until they were finally commanded and cajoled to climb the grassy hill where the flagpole stood. Rachel moved over to where her group was assigned to stand.

She only wished she'd gone to Tracy's camp. The only reason she hadn't was because Tiffany wanted to come back here again this year. But she should have gone to Tracy's camp. She'd had a fun night with Tracy.

Tiffany probably hadn't gotten around to telling her yet. But Tracy was real nice.

The flag was raised, the Pledge of Allegiance said, then Mr. Holter, the bald-headed camp owner-director, in shorts that reached his knees, made the usual announcements: a counselor who was out sick that day (cheers), a change in the lunch menu (cheers and boos), they should be courteous to the Camp Mowa team that was coming over this morning, and about tomorrow.

"Those of you who are signed up for tomorrow's overnight must remember to bring your sleeping bag—we don't have any extras. And remember to bring a flashlight. If your parents permit it, feel free to bring candy, cookies—enough, if I may suggest it, so that you can share with each other. Those of you who are not staying overnight should tell your parents that you will be driven home at the regular hour."

The groups were drifting away now to go to their activities. Tiffany, with a quick glance at her, said with a frown, "You gonna bring your big flashlight?"

"Yes." Tiffany always liked to borrow her flashlight—it could shine ten blocks away.

They walked silently. Then, though she hadn't intended to, Rachel said, "Why did you tell?"

They stopped. Tiffany said, her face flushed under her tan, "Tell what?"

"You know."

"Tell what?"

"You know." She didn't want to cry, but she was starting to.

"Oh. That. Well, it's funny, isn't it funny?"

"What's funny?"

"I don't know, whatever you said. She works for some company that owns it. I don't know what you said, is that what you said?"

"You didn't say she does it?"

"No."

She was lying, Rachel felt, and anyway a good friend wouldn't have said anything. But she wanted to believe her, and other girls were starting to come up. Mindy said excitedly, "George is going to bring cigarettes."

Tiffany said, "You want to get sick again?"

"I didn't get sick from that, you got sick. And Rachel got sick."

"I didn't get sick," Rachel said. "I took one puff and I coughed. I hate cigarettes."

It felt good to be part of it all, but as they walked in a group to archery she still felt like an outsider.

Overnight was the biggest thing in camp, bigger even than color war, which she looked on as really for kids. This was a cookout and night swims and a bonfire and everyone up all night telling funny stories and scary stories, and sometimes the boys sneaking over and throwing clattering pans on the roof, or they going over there and pulling a kid along in his sleeping bag.

190

But she didn't know if she'd go. Her Mom still seemed so worried, and she hated leaving her alone again all night.


LYNN FILLED THE bird-feeder—squirrels had gotten into it again—then stood looking around the garden.

Everything could be so perfect. It was a beautiful morning, Rachel was healthy, there was Glenn, there were good movies to see, shows, long rides to take. It could be perfect. And what was maddening was that she'd brought it all on herself.

She kept reminding herself that Wing didn't know her name, wouldn't have called her Dawn if he did. And without it, how could he find out where she lived?

True, but still . . .

Say a week, make it two weeks—if he didn't show up in two weeks she was free of it all. Then, dear God, she could take off with Rachel somewhere and not be afraid of coming back.

In the house, she heard the familiar sounds from the mailbox. She looked through the mail quickly—if not bills, junk—then was pleased to see a letter to Rachel from Jon. The return address was in London, which she hoped meant he was having a play produced there.

"You don't care if I ever write again, you don't give a goddam. All you want is me in a three-piece suit, and the bucks." How many times had she heard that, and variations?

She put the letter on the dining room table.

A few minutes later, she got a call from Glenn. He was just about to leave his apartment, was going out of town overnight.

"I just wanted to call and say hello. Hello."

"Hello." She managed a smile.

"And how are you?"

"Good. You?"

"Good. Look, I've only got a few minutes. Let me kiss you goodbye."

"I wish."

"What do you mean you wish? I'm holding you real close right now and I'm going to kiss you."

She was suddenly aware of silence. She frowned.

"I'm still holding you," he said quietly. "Do you know?"

191

Her eyes, almost without her knowing, had closed.

"Yes," she said, nodding.

HE DROVE SLOWLY along Lynn Shephard's street, looking for the address. It should be soon. Suddenly he came to a stretch of five or six houses where he couldn't see addresses. He circled the block quickly and came back even slower, trying to detect numbers through bushes, trees. Nothing on this one, couldn't see any here, nothing goddam it here, nothing—But now he saw an address that told him he was almost there, one or two houses more. And there it was, a brick and frame house, with a driveway and garage.

He circled the block again, and sat facing the house.

But was she really Dawn? He still didn't know for sure. He'd called her three times, four, but the line was busy—the whore kept talking. And then he'd realized he shouldn't even call, that if she heard someone hang up she would know and run.

He wondered was she in the house. There was no car in the driveway, but maybe it was in the garage. He wished he could just go up there and ring the bell. But if it was her, what then?

All he wanted right now was to know. But he couldn't sit here too much longer, just hoping he'd see her. There were too many cops out.

He kept staring at the house, wondering what it looked like in there. Probably a bunch of whore shit! But there was a hollowness in him as he kept looking . . . That beautiful, fine face? A whore?

A few cars went by. Across the street a woman was walking her dog. She was letting it sniff forever on someone's lawn. A yellow bus came to a stop at the corner and several kids got off. He watched as two of them, both girls, stood there talking for a while. Now one of them was walking this way.

He frowned, sitting up a little straighter, as she looked at the house, then turned up the driveway. Her daughter? Sister?

She looked very young—maybe ten.

The age of his Freddie.

She had a daughter the age of his Freddie? Even that?

He was trying to think of what to do when he heard a car

starting up. Now it was coming out of the driveway, barely visible above the large hedge that bordered it. It backed into the street toward him, then pulled off the other way.

A dark blue two-door. Hers.

He watched as it drove off.

He wished he'd brought his gun. Oh, did he wish it. He'd follow them and pull them to the side somewhere, and he'd make her suffer the way he was suffering.

He let his head go back. His chest was heaving. A world without Dawn? No more?

The ache was back, was spreading.

Maybe—God, just maybe—if she really knew him, she'd give him a chance. . .

# 25

RACHEL CAME DOWNSTAIRS, carrying her sleeping bag and an overnight bag. Lynn said, "Did you pack the chips, the cookies?"

"Yes." It came out like a sigh.

"Rach, I don't know why you're not looking forward to it. You were. It's fun."

"It's for *kids.*"

"Oh, come on."

"It is. It's for kids."

"Well, you're a kid," she smiled. "Be grateful."

"*Mom.*"

"*Rach.*"

"It's not funny."

"Honey, look, I've told you. What did I tell you? If you don't want to stay, don't stay."

"I know."

"So? I don't know what else to say. Just take the things in case. I don't want you to be sorry. Just call me either way."

Rachel seemed to be thinking it over. Then she hoisted her things. Lynn walked her to the door. She said, "I want you to have fun. That's all I want."

"I know."

Lynn kissed her. "Hey, I love you."

"I love you."

"Call me."

"I will." Rachel started to walk off.

"It's a beautiful day," Lynn said. "Have fun."

"I will."

Closing the door, she felt like pressing her forehead against it. Rachel, she was sure, was reacting to her, was picking up vibes. And yet there was probably more to it than that. There were Rachel's own problems, whatever they were, though certainly Jon was one of them. His letter yesterday, enclosing a draft for a hundred and fifty dollars, was so typical. How much he loved her. And yet, again, it was the first in months.

Well, she couldn't do anything about Jon, but she could about herself. She opened the newspaper and, after a brief glance at the front page, went to help-wanted. She checked off a few listings and circled an ad for a copywriter by an agency she was already listed with. That was depressing, but she'd call anyway.

Putting down the paper, she found herself wondering about something she hadn't thought of—if Thomas Hadley had ever told the girls why she'd left. She should have done it herself, should have at least told Manya; shouldn't have just disappeared. But she'd wanted to disappear, to cut herself off completely from it, from all of them; to try to bury everything about it.

She would call Manya at home this evening.

Funny, though, she reflected, she didn't know her phone number or even her exact address. Or even, now that she was trying to think of it, Master Surveys's phone number. But then it came to her.

Tina answered. "Oh, hon. How're you doing?"

"Good, how are you?"

"Oh my, did you miss a mess."

Some kids broke in a couple nights ago and vandalized the place, upstairs, downstairs, ripped everything apart, ruined the files. You should see what they did to the walls, the pictures, the chairs, the desks. God knows what all they destroyed or stole.

"How do you know it was kids?"

"Oh, it's kids all right. That's what the cops say. Teenagers, probably. It's a real mess. All the girls are working from home—

it'll probably be a couple more days. I'm the only one upstairs."

Are you lucky you missed it, she said again.

SHE SAT DAZEDLY by the phone.

It had to be him. It was too coincidental. She had to call the police, there was no other way.

But how could she? Rachel knowing, Glenn knowing, everyone knowing—and maybe it really was kids. That was the sort of thing kids do, go in some place, tear it apart just to tear it apart. Or say it was the worst, that it was him, what could he find? He wouldn't know her name. And ripping the walls, all of that—that would be his frustration.

But there was one thing—she had changed her mind. She was going away with Rachel.

TIFFANY'S HANDS FLEW to her hips. "What do you mean? What do you mean you're not going to stay?"

"I didn't say I'm not going to stay, I just said I was just thinking," Rachel said.

A few other girls on their way to the pool gathered around. Tiffany's eyes flared. "What do you mean you're thinking?"

"I'm just thinking, that's all. I was just saying."

"You're gay, you know that? You really are."

"I didn't say I'm not going to stay," Rachel said, starting to walk on.

"Well, are you *staying?*"

"Yes!"

"I swear, you must be going to get your peer-iod." And some of the girls giggled.

It was free-swim time—no instruction. The pool raged with children. Rachel sat on the side, just her feet in the water. But the swim counselor began looking her way, so she slid in. She stood there, then did a slow sidestroke for a few feet, then stopped and stood again. She shielded her face from some splashing, annoyed. She wanted to stay, she wanted to be home, she didn't know what she wanted. And that damn Tiffany made her feel stupid. She *hated* her.

Later, dressing for softball, she stood up after putting on her sneakers, but suddenly had to sit down again. The room had

197

started to turn; it was better now, but she was sweating and had that feeling that maybe she might have to throw up. Most of the girls were drifting out of the bunk. Soon Carol, her counselor, said from the doorway, "Rachel?"

"I don't feel well."

She came over. "What's the matter, darling?"

"I feel sick to my stomach."

"Oh my. Let's get you to the nurse."

The nurse asked quickly if she wanted the toilet. She shook her head—she'd throw up if she looked at it. The nurse had her lie down on a cot.

"You tell me if you have to vomit," she said.

"Can I call my mother?"

"Wouldn't you like to wait a little? I'm sure it'll pass, you'll feel better."

"I want to tell her something."

The nurse dialed the number, and Rachel went over to her desk. After she spoke to her mother, she lay down again. Yes, of course come home.

A nice breeze was blowing through the screens. She closed her eyes. In the distance were the tiny sounds of the kids. Soon she began to feel better.

WHILE SHE WAS dialing, Lynn lowered the phone. She thought she'd heard the slight sound of scraping near the trash cans, thought it might be Rachel coming through the back. But she heard nothing more.

"Hello," someone said on the other end of the line.

"Yes, this is Mrs. Shephard. My daughter's a camper—Rachel. I'm a little concerned because she's usually home by now, and she wasn't feeling well."

"Hold on." Then, "No, don't worry. The bus left late—one of the kids who was supposed to go home didn't want to miss the overnight and they had to go looking for him."

"I see. I thought maybe Rachel decided to stay."

"No, I see her checked off for the bus. She should be home any minute."

"Okay, thank you."

198

She shook her head to herself as she stood up. On top of everything else today, that. But thank God.

She went to one of the front windows and peered toward the bus stop, though she couldn't see it from here. It had always been her way of urging people into view—her little cousins, years ago, when they were expected over; her mother and father; Jon; Rachel, always, when her school bus was late. She went into the kitchen and resurrected the morning paper, which she just remembered she'd tied up with several others to take outside. She wanted it because she'd seen several interesting rentals for houses in Ocean City, two with outboards and docks.

"Rach?"

She'd thought she heard her come in, but she obviously hadn't; there was just the empty center hall in front of her. She walked quickly to the door, sure that Rachel was having trouble with the lock, perhaps had forgotten her key. She opened the door—then with a hoarse cry pressed her whole body against it, feet sliding, trying to hold it closed, then having to let go. Suddenly he was toppling forward, like something released.

She whirled and ran to the kitchen, trying to get to the door, but his hand reached out behind her and grabbed her wrist. She tore free, but had to scramble back from the door, he was blocking her way. Staring at him across the kitchen, she started inching over to the hall to run to the front door again, but he moved slowly with her, crimson-faced and slightly hunched toward her, in a crumpled sport jacket, tie pulled to the side. His eyes, wilder than before, stayed on her. She stopped, her heart exploding.

"Don't—don't—hurt me." She held out her arm as though it was clutching a knife. "Don't hurt me."

He seemed to be struggling just to slow his breathing. "I—won't. But just—just—stay." He started to come closer.

"Please." She kept thrusting out her arm, started to inch toward the door. "Don't. Don't."

He stopped. He kept staring; each breath seemed to sear him. "Why—didn't you let me talk? Why did you drive away? Why'd you run? Didn't have to run."

"I—" But there were no words. She shook her head quickly.

"Why did you run? Why did you run?"

199

She kept shaking her head. And then suddenly thought of Rachel.

She'd be home soon!

"Why? Why?"

"I—I was scared. I—told you. I don't know you, didn't know what—"

"Don't know me!" His eyes grew even wider. "All the times we've talked! You told me how good and kind I was. Told me you thought of me . . . Don't *know* me!"

Everything was wrong! Whatever she'd say! And Rachel would be here any minute!

"Everything was a lie, wasn't it? Whatever you said."

"No. No." She was shaking her head.

"What wasn't a lie? Tell me."

"I—" But she couldn't think; her brain was frozen. "Please. I-I'll go with you. Anywhere you want."

"'Wing, you're so good, Wing you're so great, Wing I've been thinking of you.' All a lie! And I thought of you all the time. Needed you, loved you. Offered everything I have. All a lie!"

"No." The man was mad! "No." She was shaking her head again, but her eyes were looking for something to throw, to push between them, to stab with, to beat—

"In my head." His hands started to go to his head. "You put yourself in my head."

The little candleholder. No. That plate—

"And then you run from me. I said I wanted to talk to you—you smiled, you lied again, you said wait, you would—"

No, not the plate. The sugar bowl. Just in reach, on the shelf. Throw it. But it had to hit his face.

"You're in my head and it's all a lie."

"Wing, it isn't, I'll go with you, we'll talk, we'll—"

"All a lie, you're—"

And suddenly she had the bowl in her hand, took a step forward and flung it in his face. He fell back in an explosion of sugar, grabbing at his face, and she was at the door, turning the knob. She had it open and was running. She ran toward the rear street, then along it, trying to scream, unable to. Then she stopped as if impaled, hands to her mouth.

200

Oh God! The bus!

She could see it ahead, picking up speed. It had left the stop.

She whirled, ran back toward the house, stumbled once, ran.

Then all at once she was running along her own street, screaming.

That cry—that terrible cry of Rachel's she'd heard from the house!

# 26

SCREAMING, RACHEL FLUNG her arms over her face as he kept shoving her from the doorway across the room. She fell onto the sofa, sagged over on her side.

"Shut up! Shut up!" But she couldn't stop. Now his fingers were in her hair, yanking her upright. "Shut up, you hear me, shut up!"

She began nodding wildly, and he gradually released her. She sank her face in her hands, biting the flesh, the screams moans now, gasps.

He broke from the sofa to look out a window, then another. She kept her face covered, kept biting, feeling a scream coming, fighting it. Where was Mama? She began sobbing. Where was Mama, was she dead?

And it was as though he'd heard.

"Your mother's a no good cocksucking whore!"

She dug her face even harder into her hands.

Mama. Mama.


SCREAMING, SHE RAN up the Hunsicker's driveway, began pounding on their door. Where were they? Her baby! She kept pounding, ringing, then ran across the lawn to the next neighbor, began pounding again, screaming, ringing. Where was everyone? Her baby!

She raced back to the sidewalk, started to run to her house, stopped. Mrs. Norlund and a scattering of other neighbors were converging on her.

"The police! Call the police! Someone's got my Rachel!"

Mrs. Norlund took her by the shoulders. "Who? Who's got Rachel?"

"In the house! A man!"

She started to run to her house, but Mrs. Norlund grabbed hold of her. "Don't. God's sake! Wait for the police! Someone's calling!"

She grabbed at her head. Her Rachel! The neighbors were standing about, wide-eyed, talking quickly to one another; others kept streaming in. Her house was only a few houses away, but she couldn't see it from here, from the same side of the street—there were too many trees and bushes on the lawns. She ran into the street, but another neighbor caught hold of her.

"Please," Lynn cried. "Please."

The hands fell away, but she was barely aware of it. Her hands were to her mouth as she stared at her house.

Sirens now, in the distance, and the first police cars began pulling up. A uniformed officer, pausing briefly among the neighbors, came over; others were ordering people away, gesturing, shouting.

He said, "Your youngster's in there?"

She nodded, began crying.

"Who's got her?"

"I—I know him but I don't really know him. Calls himself Wing. Pushed his way in."

"He got a gun?"

"I don't know, I didn't see it."

He and another officer started walking up the middle of the street to the house. They stood looking at it. She started to take a few steps toward them, but suddenly there was a shot and they started to kneel, reaching for their guns, then came running back. One of them took her by the arm and hurried her over to the sidewalk. She tried to tear from him.

204

"Where—where was the shot? He shot!"

"At us, not her! Come on, stop it!" Mrs. Norlund came over and put her arms around her. The officer said, "In the house! Get back in the house!" He was already starting to move away, his hand on his holster. Mrs. Norlund started to lead her to her house, but she pulled away and stood on the lawn, her hands to her face.

Police cars kept pulling in, parking at angles. Officers stood or crouched behind them. She bit at her hand, her body shaking convulsively. Mrs. Norlund had her arm around her again, tightened it.

She'd done this, she'd done it to Rachel, she'd done this herself!

A squat, bowlegged man carrying a bulletproof vest strode toward her. "Mrs. Shephard?"

She nodded quickly, as though he were bringing her hope.

"Delaney. Captain Delaney." His face was flushed, tense; he looked genuinely sorry for her. "Let's go where we can talk."

"I don't want to go in."

"It's very important. Please."

Mrs. Norlund led them into the house, then left them alone in the living room. Delaney, about fifty, with graying red hair and a seamed face, put his vest on the sofa next to him. The top two buttons of his short-sleeved shirt were open, so that a religious medal showed as he leaned toward her. He waited as she kept gasping, then he said, "Look, let me first tell you something about myself."

He'd been a cop for twenty-six years, a detective for the last twenty-one. He had a lot of experience in "hostage situations." And he had, Mrs. Shephard, eight kids.

She looked at him. She was able to nod, still gasping. Somehow that was a touch of comfort.

He said, "Who is he? Do you know him?"

"I—only know him as—as Wing. Wing. That's all I know."

"I hear he just broke in."

"He pushed his way in. I was waiting for Rachel and I opened the door and he pushed his way in. I managed to run out—I ran out the back. I threw something at him and I ran."

"And your daughter, where was she?"

"She came home after I ran out. I shouldn't have run." Her fingers dug under her hair. "I should have stayed."

205

"No, no. No. Don't. Don't do that to yourself. You did right. Now tell me, how do you know him?"

She closed her eyes, biting at her lip. Her Rachel was in there with a crazy man, he was going to kill her—yet it was hard to say. "I—work at one of those places—men call you—you talk?... You know"—she opened her eyes—"you talk?"

He didn't seem to understand.

"You know—they—they call you—you talk?"

He still seemed puzzled. Then he said, hesitantly, "You mean those sex calls?"

She nodded quickly. "And he's been calling. And he wanted to meet me, see me. And several days ago—I can't remember the day—I can't think—he showed up at the parking lot."

"Where's this?"

"It's called Master Surveys. Or Phone Friend—it's part of Master Surveys . . . I'm sorry," she said, crying again. Then, trying to control her gasping, "He showed up there. I was getting in my car."

"Did he threaten you?"

"No. But I was scared. He said—he said—he wanted to talk to me. Said he needed me, loved me . . . Offered to buy me things. Like—it was something crazy—like he had fifteen thousand dollars—I don't remember. Said he wanted to see me, talk to me. I—I jumped in the car. I should have stayed. Should have gone with him."

"Let me ask—I'm not sure I understand. How'd you manage to get out of the house if he had a gun?"

"I didn't see a gun, he wasn't holding a gun. I ran into the kitchen, and he kept saying I lied to him, but he didn't have a gun. I—I don't know what he wanted. Maybe I—didn't talk to him right. I—I don't even remember talking to him, what I said, except I'd go with him—I wanted him out of there. I should have talked, pleaded—why didn't I talk? Or just listened. Listened. But I threw something, I was afraid for Rachel."

"How did he know where you live? Did you tell him?"

"No! He didn't even know my name! I don't even know how he got to Masters. I never told him. I don't know." Then, suddenly remembering, "I didn't tell you. They were broken into a couple days ago. Maybe he got my address there. I don't know."

"How old would you say he is?"

"In his thirties, I guess, I don't know."

"Did he ever tell you anything about himself? Where he works? Anything?"

"I don't remember, I don't think so. Can't I," she pleaded, "go out?" She wanted to be closer. Even the lawn was better.

"This can be very, very important, believe me. If we have any idea who he is, maybe we can get somebody to help us—his minister, priest, wife, someone. Now, can you think of anything he said about himself?"

"I—really can't. Except—he said something about winning an award for helping people."

"Did he say what kind of award? Who gave it?"

"No. Captain, please—"

"Just one more thing." He wanted the phone number at her house—he was going to try to talk to the guy from the command van. The big thing in these cases was to maintain contact, keep these guys talking, try not to provoke them further, give them time to cool off. He stood up and started to put on the vest, when suddenly he whirled. She'd heard two little pops, which she hadn't realized until now were gunfire. She raced after Delaney to the door.

"Stay here!" He almost pushed her back as he opened the door. But she ran out to the driveway. He was running, hunched over, to the barricade of cars. Mrs. Norlund ran to her.

"Come inside!"

Lynn pushed her away and went closer to the street. Oh Rachel, Rachel!

Please let her be alive! Please!

IT WAS LIKE a frieze—the officers, holding revolvers and huge rifles, fixed into position behind the cars. At each corner, in the still-bright sunshine, were crowds of people; several men, a few carrying cameras, a couple with TV cameras on their shoulders, were moving cautiously up the sidewalks.

About ten minutes later Delaney made his way back to her.

She said, almost too terrified to ask, "The shots."

"She's all right," he said. "I was just talking to him. He fired out, we didn't fire back. He has a—real thing about cops. Look, we've

207

got to talk. Let's go in." In the living room, with Mrs. Norlund looking on, he said, "He wants to talk to you."

She stared at him, then started for the door. He grabbed her wrist. "No, you're not going there. No. Christ, no."

She stared at him again, then looked at Mrs. Norlund. She pulled her arm back, then walked quickly to the kitchen, to the phone.

"Wait, wait," Delaney said. "Wait. This guy's like dynamite with a lit fuse. He doesn't want to talk to cops—we're bringing in a psychologist. But he wants to talk to you. Now listen to me. Just listen to him. Don't argue with him, don't contradict him, just let him talk. He'll probably rant and rave and make all kinds of threats. You're not going to get him to calm down and walk out of there with one call. It may take dozens. But hopefully he'll start talking, and that's the thing. If there's the opportunity, you might say you're sorry you ran out, but you were scared. You're sorry. But he might not even give you a chance to say it. Or it might only get him madder. Just let him keep talking. You might say things like 'I understand,' just to keep him talking, to make him feel you feel what he's saying, that you're not arguing with him. We've got to keep him talking if it takes three weeks."

"Let me call him. Please." But suddenly, as she started to dial, she couldn't remember her number. She had to put down the phone, had to think. Now she was dialing again, her hand trembling.

The phone kept ringing.

Then all at once, "Yes! Yes!"

It was a crazed voice—not the voice she knew. "It's—me."

"You!" Wing screamed. "You! I'm gonna kill your little bastard, hear me? You come over here or I'm gonna kill her!"

"Yes." She was crying. "Don't hurt her. Please."

"You! You hear me, you!"

And the phone went dead.

Mrs. Norlund hurried over to hold her. But she didn't want to be held. She clutched her face. "He's going to kill her!"

"Honey, please—" Mrs. Norlund kept trying to put her arms around her.

"He's going to kill her."

"Honey, it's going to work out all right. You'll see."

She let herself be led into the living room. She sagged onto a chair. But though she looked from Mrs. Norlund to Delaney, her eyes were taking in the door.

Delaney said, "Do you think you could do this? Tell him we won't let you come? Put it on us?"

She stood up, began to pace. Then all at once she was at the door, had it open, was running down the steps toward the street. But arms caught her from behind. She struggled to tear free. "He wants—me. I'm the one he wants."

"He'll kill both of you." Delaney held on tightly as she kept thrashing.

"No."

"Kill both of you."

Her body slowly went limp. But he held her just as hard.

"We can't let you stay here any more."

"Oh no, please."

"We can't take the chance."

"Please. I won't any more." Her head sagged back against him; she just wanted to be near her. "I swear."

# 27

ALONE WITH HER in the kitchen, Delaney, his face fiery, shouted, "You want her killed? Is that what the hell you want?"

She shook her head dazedly, staring at him, crying, from the chair.

"That's what the hell you were doing! That's exactly what you were doing! No, no," he said, waving his hands to himself, "you ain't staying here, you can't stay here. You're getting out of here."

"No."

"No, hell."

"You can't! You can't make me leave!"

"That," he said quietly, "is what you think. Look, I know what you're going through, but I can't spend a hell of a lot of time thinking about it. I'm here for one thing—to get your daughter out of there alive. That's the only thing I got in my head. And you're gonna screw it up."

"I won't, I promise. I promised, I swore."

"Now you just listen to me," he said, sitting down. "You listen"—he pointed a stubby finger—"to what I got to say. You staying the hell out of there, you staying alive, is the kid's best insurance policy, maybe her only insurance policy. Do you understand?"

She began to nod, then shook her head, then held her temples. His words seemed to enter a whirlpool in her head; she couldn't hold onto them. And entering too were the sounds from outside—officers yelling to each other from behind cars, sirens coming and going, the bellow of a bullhorn ordering people to stay back.

He said, "Don't you understand? He wants you—and as long as you're alive, your daughter's got the best chance of staying alive. But you go over there, he's all this worked up, you're dead, she's dead. You got that? You understand?"

She nodded quickly. "But—you're not going to break in there shooting—"

"That's the last damn resort. But we're not going to miss any opportunity he gets careless and steps in front of a window."

"But my daughter—"

"We've got real sharpshooters out there."

He slid a stick of gum into his mouth; his cheek bulged instantly as he chewed. He sat thoughtfully, then said, "You up to calling him again?"

"Please, yes."

"All right. Look, I don't want him to think you broke your word. He's on fire enough. So keep stalling him. Tell him you want to come, you've tried, but we won't let you. You're going to keep trying, but he's got to give you time. But—and this is tricky— don't promise you'll be there, just that you'll try."

Lynn nodded, trying to catch her breath; didn't know if she could even talk. She waited until Delaney had time to get to an extension, then dialed. It rang several times.

"Yes!"

"Wing?" There was silence. "Wing?"

"Yes! Yes!"

"Wing"—tears brimmed her eyes—"they won't let me, the police won't let me come. I tried but they stopped me. I—I'm just down the street, but they're in the house, they're watching me. I will, I don't know how, but I'm going to try, I will." Again silence. "Wing?"

"You bitch." His voice was low now, hoarse. "You filth. You think I won't do it?" A shot rang out. "That's in the ceiling! Next one's in her fucking heart you're not here. Hear me?"

212

And the phone was dead.

Lynn started to run to Delaney, but he was there first. He took her by both arms. "Come on, sit down, sit down, come on . . . That's it."

"What do we do?" She stared at him imploringly.

"Don't make any more calls," he said, gesturing. "That's number one. He's a powder keg. Look, I'm going to the van—the psychologist should be here any minute, he's very good at this. But I can't leave you here. You can't stay here."

"No. I'm staying."

"I said you can't stay here."

"No!"

"Don't tell me no."

He looked at her. Then he said, "No monkey business? You'll stay the fuck here?"

The word jolted her. She felt herself nodding dazedly.

He took a glass out of a cabinet and filled it with water. He drank quickly. As he set down the glass he said, "It's just that it doesn't take too much to fuck these things up."

She stared at him. It had come out all at once—what he really thought of her, that he could say anything to her.

He said, "I'll be at the van, but I'll be back."

She watched as he walked off. "Mr. Delaney."

He turned. She had no idea what she wanted to say. All she knew was that she was crying again. He stood there, looking at her, the chewing gradually stopping. First his eyes, then his whole face, softened.

"We're going to do our damn best," he said quietly.

RACHEL SCREAMED AT the shot, slammed her hands over her ears, sobbing. He whirled, the revolver aimed squarely at her. He held it to her face, then pulled back slightly and sat on the floor, staring at her. His chest heaved.

"She's a no good whore, and you're the whore of a whore!"

She tried not to hear, tried to hide her whole face in the sofa, under the cover of her arms. She wished she could kill him. If only Daddy was here, if he only knew she was here, he'd bring a gun and kill him. That time they'd gone to that resort in the mountains, he went skeet shooting and shot every one. She remem-

213

bered him standing there, tall, aiming, bang, and there was always a burst of white dust in the sky. . . He'd kill him!

The phone was ringing again—he was screaming into it he didn't talk to cops, and she could hear the slam of the receiver. It rang again and the same thing. Then there was a bellowing voice from outside that made her sit up part way.

"We're not going to hurt you. We're not here to hurt you. We only want to help you."

He was wriggling on his stomach toward a window, but at an angle so that he could still see her. He raised his hand up quickly, fired twice through the glass, and wriggled back. The bellowing stopped, but then started again. He took out a small box of bullets and began reloading. He fired at the window again.

He looked up at her from the floor.

"Your mother's filth!"

She clamped her hands on her ears, but the words kept coming through.

Evil, rotten, filth, witch, fucker, sucker, whore. "Fucks the world on the phone!"

She squeezed harder, crying.

THE INSTANT LYNN walked outside she was aware of a terrifying change in the light. The colors had softened; there were faint shadows. Oh God, don't let it get dark.

She started down the driveway toward the sidewalk when a uniformed officer Delaney had left in the house with her said, "Ma'am, you'll have to stay back here." A middle-aged man, he always looked at her with the saddest eyes.

She had to come back to the part of the driveway between Mrs. Norlund's house and her neighbor's. It was maddening that she couldn't even see her . . . lawn, something. She whirled and went to Mrs. Norlund's backyard, the officer following quickly. She tried to see her house through the bushes and trees; it was five houses away. She thought she could make out a window, one of the upstairs' windows. Rachel's room.

Lips quivering, she raised herself on her toes, as if somehow she could look in. For some stupid reason—she didn't want memories now, she wanted Rachel!—she found herself thinking of the

214

time Rachel, she must have been all of five, made a "kite" out of some pieces of newspaper and string and flung it out the window into the wind. She'd cried until Jon climbed onto the roof to get it and, sitting with her on the bottom of the ladder, explained why it wouldn't work, that he would buy her one as soon as the stores opened in the morning. Or the time—it was all that window!— Rachel was sick for a week or so and Jon, who had a good idea of the one Rachel wanted, surprised her up in that room with her first two-wheeler.

She wiped at her eyes as she walked toward the front again. Mrs. Norlund had stepped out to the driveway.

"I tried to reach Glenn. They say he's out somewhere."

She didn't care where he was, here, away on a trip, even over there where several TV vans were parked behind wooden barricades.

"Come inside, please," Mrs. Norlund said. "Try to lie down, sit down."

"I can't."

"Please." Tears began trickling down her bony, aristocratic face.

"Oh, Mrs. Norlund." Lynn held onto her. She wanted to sob out: I did it, I thought I could step in shit and just walk away. But she just held onto her a little longer.

"You'll see," Mrs. Norlund said, stroking her back, "it's going to be all right."

Several officers, with Delaney in the middle, were walking quickly across the lawn to her. The others stayed back as Delaney came up to her.

He said, "I've got a name for you. Do you know a Leon Owens?"

"No."

Well, they'd been checking on cars parked in the neighborhood and they found one that didn't belong to anyone around here. It was registered to Owens.

"No one's at his house, but neighbors say his wife recently left him—they've got a kid about ten or eleven. And he's a nurse." Delaney understood the sudden look in her eyes. "I know, helping people. Well, look, I want you to know where we stand. We've learned where his wife lives—she's not in, we're trying to reach her. And there's a mother somewhere. So, if it's him we'll see what they can do. Okay? I'll let you know as soon as I know anything."

She watched him walk off, the other officers with him.

# 28

LEON FOUGHT THE pistons in him. He wanted to keep moving—go over there, come back here, run upstairs. But he kept braking himself, made himself stay kneeling on the floor, the longest he'd been in one spot.

From here, away from the windows, he could see in the foyer mirror a reflection of one of the police cars. And watch that little fuck at the same time. His Colt was fully loaded, and he had both boxes of bullets on the floor. He only wished he'd brought along Freddie's Winchester too.

To throw something at him and run! *I don't know you,* and to throw something!

He'd even gone there in a jacket and tie. To impress her. With everything he knew about her, the cards, everything, to try one more time.

And then—*Don't know you.*

Why hadn't he gone for his gun right then and just fired at the filth?

His eyes kept darting toward the door, then down the hall to the back door, then to the mirror again. Maybe he ought to go upstairs in case they came crashing through the doors. But fuck 'em. He could still pop off the fucking kid, and some of them; the important thing.

"She's a fucking whore! A whore!"

His throat, even his head, hurt from his screaming. But he couldn't stop it. There were too many words in his head, too many things screaming to be screamed out. And he wanted her to know—he wanted that whore of a mother in her head too.

He stared at her, curled up on the sofa.

Stop your fucking crying!

He reached for his jacket on the floor and wiped his face with the sleeve. He flung it away and stared at the mirror again. It had grayed with the evening.

Daddy, Freddie said, I want to go on again.

Why now? To come back now?

Daddy, I want to go on again.

It was the crying. Daddy, I want to go on again, and Freddie had cried too.

It had been in Disneyland, and he'd gone with Freddie on that crazy space ride. It had bounced his brain around in his skull, but Daddy I want to go on again, and the crying, and he could never bear to see him cry, and so he'd gone with him again. And afterward Della, who'd wanted no part of that, went on the submarine ride with them, and afterward they'd had hot dogs, and that was one of the times he'd given someone his camera to take their picture.

But why now?

But they'd been good days, such good days! They'd made up for all the bad days, that sister shit, that fucking sister shit, and being the only one of the guys in the car who couldn't make it in the whore house, though he never said it, then being the only one who wasn't married. And then all those good days, a kid of his own, a wife, to be able to walk with a baby carriage, to be proud. . .

But then that witch!

He felt a sting of tears, and he ran a fast arm across his eyes.

"She's a whore! A whore!"

He spun toward her again.

Stop your fucking crying, you little fuck.

*Kids.*

218

*Kids!*

Thank you, Daddy, for the bike. Thank you, Daddy, for the radio. Thank you, Daddy, thank you, Daddy, thank you, Daddy.

I want to be with my Mommy!

"She fucked on the phone! You hear me? You hear me?"

He looked at the mirror again, chest pumping. He could see the reflection of a street lamp, and in the deepening night he felt for the first time a little pinch of fear. But it coursed away with a rush of blood. What he did, what he used to do, the calls—they all knew. The cops knew, and everyone in their homes knew, and Della knew, and Freddie and Maggie and Dr. Blay and everyone who voted for him and all of his neighbors. They knew.

He wanted to die, but he wasn't going to die alone.

SHE STAYED OUT on the driveway; it was as though being outside would bring Delaney back faster.

"What time's it?"

"Almost nine. Honey, it's only about a half hour—"

No, about an hour. More. No, it was no good. No.

Spotlights illuminated her house now; they isolated it even more. One of the figures crouched nearby held a walkie-talkie as well as a rifle. In the distance was the sound of horns from cars jammed up and forced to detour.

No good, it was no good, he would have been back—

She felt a sudden ripple of dizziness. Mrs. Norlund, her arm through hers, apparently sensed something, looked at her quickly.

Lynn said, "I'm all right." But she wasn't. The dizziness had passed, but her legs felt like they were going to give. The officer assigned to her was looking at her too; he had never once said a word, just kept looking sad. Lynn said, "I had better go in."

She sank onto a chair, head back. She felt clammy, exhausted; everything seemed to have stopped in her but her heart. Mrs. Norlund rushed off for a wet towel; Lynn waved it away. "I'm all right. I just got a little weak."

She closed her eyes. Mrs. Norlund said, "I don't know where Glenn can be."

Yes, get your scoop. The true, inside story. The lady I knew. . .

219

She stood up quickly at the sound of the doorbell. But Mrs. Norlund got there first. From the voices they were reporters—the police must have let them through, or they got through. The voices soon died as Mrs. Norlund closed the door. She came back, saying nothing.

The next time it was Delaney. His face was sweat-lined, almost scarlet.

"I just stopped to tell you. It's him. So I'll keep you informed. Right now there's nothing to report."

She stared at him. "How do you know it's him? Someone talked to him? Please tell me."

His face looked pained. "His wife." He gestured helplessly. "Some screaming. Hung up. We're trying to locate his mother—she's out. And there's a minister he used to like."

She reached behind her for the arm of her chair, sank down again.

"Look, the psychologist is in contact with him. And he might just burn himself out too. The longer it goes on, the better the chance of that . . . Okay?"

She was staring straight ahead.

"So, I'll be back to you."

Mrs. Norlund kneeled next to her when he left.

"Honey, is there someone I can call? Someone you want with you?"

Still staring ahead, she shook her head slowly. But her hand came out and rested on Mrs. Norlund's.

"A doctor? Someone?"

"No." Lynn looked at her. "No."

Mrs. Norlund sat down across from her. Lynn looked toward the kitchen. Call him again? Beg? Plead?

She couldn't think.

It might set him off, Delaney said.


RACHEL, SLUMPED OVER on the sofa, kept trying to keep her ears covered, but her hands, her arms, hurt from squeezing so much. He kept saying everything over and over.

"Dawn. You ever hear her called Dawn? . . . I said you ever hear her called Dawn?"

She shook her head, eyes closed. He always wanted her to shake her head when he said that.

The tears were starting again.

"She'd say, 'Hi. This is Dawn. Hi. What do you want to talk about? What would you like to do to me?'"

She wished she could scratch his eyes out, hit him with her fists.

"Whore. And calls here. 'I want to talk.' *Talk.*"

Maybe she should run. Run to the door. Or jump through the window, break through the glass. And then keep running.

IF SHE COULD only make him stay on the phone long enough so she could plead with him, tell him how sorry she was for everything she did.

Mrs. Norlund said, "Can I get something for you?"

"No. Thank you, no."

If she really begged. Wing, this is Lynn. Or Leon, this is Lynn. No, Wing. And beg.

Mrs. Norlund said to the officer, "Can I get you something to eat? Something to drink?"

"No, I'm fine."

If she really begged. If she could find the kindness in him, reach that part of him that said love me, asked to be held, was proud of the award, proud of helping people. It had to be there.

She stood up, still not sure what she was going to do. Mrs. Norlund looked at her.

"I'm just going to the kitchen."

"Can I get you something?"

"No, I just can't sit still."

She looked at the phone. So tempting. Plead. My daughter. And say her name—Rachel. Rach-el. Such a beautiful, beautiful name, he'll know it's a beautiful name. And tell him—a little girl. An innocent. Whatever I did, she's an innocent. Reach him, get him to feel. And listen to him. Say yes, you're right, I'm sorry, you're right. And that everything will work out, he hasn't done anything, everyone will be with him if he lets this innocent child go.

But Delaney had said don't call him any more. Leave it to the psychologist, others, maybe he'll burn himself out—

221

But just to beg him, plead with him, tell him everything in her heart?

She dialed quickly. After the second ring she started to hang up, then lifted the phone again. It hovered near her ear as it kept ringing.

"Yes! What!"

"Wing, it's me. Please listen to me."

"Listen to you! *You?*"

"Wing"—she was crying—"please listen to me. Please."

She could hear his breathing.

"Wing, whatever I did I'm sorry. Do you hear me? I—I never meant to hurt anyone. Never. I swear. I thought—maybe even helping—"

Silence, except for his breathing.

"Wing, talk to me. Please talk to me . . . I never meant to hurt you. I didn't."

Still silence. Was she reaching him? Even a little?

"Wing, I had no reason to hurt you, I wouldn't. Whatever I did, I didn't mean—"

"Liar."

She was startled by the sudden word, even the quiet way he said it.

"Wing—"

"Liar! Liar!" His voice kept growing louder. "What you did— What you did to me! Another hour—a half hour. I swear!"

"Wing—please. She's just a child. Please. Only a child. Only twelve."

"Only twelve! What about my boy, my Freddie? Only ten."

"Wing, what did I do?"

"What did you do? Turned me against him! Drove me crazy. You made me need you. That's all I thought about. You!"

"Wing, I'm sorry."

"Sorry!"

"Oh Wing." She kept crying.

"Made me need you. 'Wing, how are you? Wing, you're good. Wing, you're great. What an honor, Wing.' Liar!"

"Oh, Wing."

222

"Drove me crazy! I had a family, had my Freddie, my Della. Now I've got nothing."

"Wing—I'm so sorry—Wing—" She was shaking with sobs.

"Sorry! You made me evil, made me filthy! Put thoughts—Made me do—All I ever wanted to do was help people! That's all I ever wanted! Just help people. You made me rotten."

"Wing—"

"You're filth! You deserve to die!"

And suddenly, as he kept screaming she began nodding compulsively. Wing, wait for me, please wait!

# 29

HANGING UP, SHE looked quickly at the kitchen door. Once she was out there, she'd cut across the backyards—the Hendersons', the Powells', the others—then up the steps to her back door. But there had to be police in her yard, behind bushes and trees. And it was floodlighted back there too. Somehow she'd have to race past them, maybe fight and claw her way past them, then reach her door before they could grab her.

First, though, to reach this door. It was only a few long strides away, but it was chained. And the officer, she was suddenly aware, had heard her. Of course he'd heard her—she'd been screaming. He had moved away from the foyer and was standing in the living room, watching her through the archway. He'd be here before she could even get off the chain.

But she was getting out. He'd have to kill her.

Throw something in the archway, a kitchen chair—he'd have to get around the chair. Or grab a kitchen knife and hold it out and swear you'll kill him if he comes closer; that, or he'd have to shoot you.

He was starting to come closer. And in that instant she just ran. She flipped off the chain and was turning the knob when his hand touched her shoulder. She flung the door back against him, her body pushing open the screen door, and ran down the steps, suddenly falling forward. She kept stumbling toward the blackness of the yard, then somehow found her balance and kept running. She plunged into bushes, flung her arms against them, and pushed through. He was crashing through bushes behind her.

She was in the next yard now, the Hendersons', this their apple tree, this the tire that hung from it. She ran toward the Powells' fence, began groping her way around it, then stumbled over something, a huge root. Her hands broke her fall, in soft dirt; she lay back against the fence, then tried to compress herself into it as a flashlight beam went on somewhere to her right. He was pulling apart bushes, shooting in the light. The beam moved slowly, probing.

She slid away from it, staring, then pressed herself flat against the dirt. The beam darted, danced, froze here and there, circled. Then the light, the sounds, were moving away.

She got to her knees, was about to rise to her feet, when she felt herself swaying. She had to feel her way back to her knees. Don't let her faint now. She stood up again, but suddenly didn't know which direction her house was, which direction she'd come from. Or whose yard this was. She thought for a frantic moment it was the Rosens', which was right too—the Powells had bought it from the Rosens. It was the house Jon had talked briefly of buying because it was cheaper, then later claimed she'd talked him out of.

She began groping her way around the fence again, to the Beckers' yard. They had spotlights on the second floor, shining down on the back of the garage, the rear steps and door, an overturned wading pool in the yard, their gas barbecue. Ahead, floodlights chalked the back of her house.

Hugging the dark fringes of the yard, she worked her way around to the Hunsickers, her next door neighbor on this side. She sagged down on her knees behind their tall fir, head down. Looking up slowly, she made out first one figure and the slant of his rifle, then two, then finally three. They were crouched behind trees and the back of her garage.

226

It would be about a thirty-yard run to her steps—through the opening over there between the bushes and the hedge, then across the lawn and the patio. And she couldn't do it. Her heart was exploding; she could hardly breathe. And her mind. For a moment she couldn't remember where the steps were, forgot that they were on the other side.

And her keys, where was her little ring of keys? She rooted through her pockets, then found them in the first pocket after all. She pinched the house key. She looked for another possible opening to her yard; just that one, from here; she couldn't see any other way. But one of the men was only a few feet from it. And even if she got by him, they'd converge on her by the time she got to the other side of the house. And even if she made that, what if the door was chained? Or the screen door was locked from the inside?

She didn't know what to do about the screen—just pull, yank—but the chain, if she could find something to break one of the windows on the door. . . . She looked around the dark ground for a broken branch, or a stone—there was always a rock, a stone, when you mowed. She began feeling around. Her hand closed on something hard, but it was only a clump of dirt. What else? She kept feeling around, then suddenly remembered the metal flower pot she usually kept outside the door. Had she taken it in, put it in the garage? She couldn't remember doing it, was sure it was still out there. Could throw it through the window.

She stared back at the house, then at the opening. It was about five yards away. The officer nearest to it was scratching the back of his neck. Surely they'd been warned she had run out of the house, might try this. . . Keeping her eyes fixed on the opening, she rose slowly to a crouch. The officer shifted position, stood up and leaned against a tree. He kept looking at the house, then turned to look toward the street, away from the opening. She ran.

She almost stumbled at the opening, but ran through it; was running across the grass now, voices suddenly yelling. She could see the steps, reached them, but toppled headlong at the first one. She kept scrambling up on her hands, then rose and pulled back the screen door. The key found the lock; she twisted and plunged in, falling to her knees.

"Wing. Wing."

The house was black except for the glare of the floodlights. And silent.

"Wing," she called down the hall. Nothing. Then, "Rachel." Her voice was breaking. "Rachel?"

The house loomed cavernous in front of her. She got up slowly.

She began walking forward, a hand on the wall. "Wing? Wing, I'm alone."

The kitchen—empty. The dining room—empty. The whole downstairs empty. She hadn't looked in the closets. But then, why the closets?

"Wing!"

He'd killed her. He'd killed himself.

"Wing! Rachel!"

"Mama."

She whirled. From upstairs. She ran to the staircase. On the top of the stairs, kneeling, a dark figure clutched Rachel with one arm, and held the other out stiffly with a gun. That arm motioned for her to come up.

She walked up slowly. He pulled Rachel back with him, motioning for her to get down on the floor, then to crawl to the front bedroom. Floodlights filled the windows, whitened the walls. But his face was in darkness. Rachel tore from him and scrambled over to her, crying. Lynn clutched her, face against her hair; kept squeezing her, then looked at him.

"Let her go. Please."

He reached in with his free hand, tried to pry Rachel from her. Lynn held on.

"Please let her go."

He stared at Lynn. Then he tilted his head slowly from side to side, as though trying to penetrate the darkness.

"Please."

He kept staring. Then he motioned with his gun hand. She didn't know what he meant. He motioned again—go back. She began to slide back with Rachel. But he motioned her in another direction, then to go still farther back. She was pressed against the bed, her arms around Rachel's head. He kept staring. Then she saw his free hand reach up. And it turned on a lamp.

228

Bright, brighter, brightest.

He stared at her—at her face, then just her eyes, her mouth, her whole face again, then slowly down the full length of her, then at her face again. He kept staring. His eyes began growing wider. He raised the gun a little higher and held it directly to her face—then with a scream swung it to Rachel's head.

Lynn leaped, arms outstretched.

A roar, and something punched through her, but her momentum carried her forward. She fell against him, felt his face, his hair, scratched at them, clawed. She tried to rise up with him, somehow knowing there was a window, white light against it; tried to lift him with her, to stand with him against it. But she felt herself failing, weakening.

"Run . . ."

Her fingers were loosening. She tried to hold on just a little longer, then began to fall, sliding down against him.

Please let her die. . . Rachel safe, but let her die. . .

She heard the noise, but didn't know what it was—the crashing sounds, the stampeding through the house. But she didn't hear the shots, or feel him fall on her.

# 30

RACHEL, SHAKING WITH sobs, pressed herself hard against Mrs. Norlund in the back of the police car as, lights sparkling, it pulled away from the curb. Cameramen ran alongside until it picked up speed. The car chased the distant sound of the ambulance siren.

"You'll see, sweetheart," Mrs. Norlund kept saying, stroking her back, "you'll see, you'll see."

No, her mother was going to die, was dead already. Wouldn't she have opened her eyes? Wouldn't she have moved, tried to sit up, turned her head?

"You'll see, you'll see."

Was dead like that—that—She clenched her fists, picturing him alive again, alive so she could pull his eyes out—

A sign Emergency, and the car turned into a driveway. Ahead, the ambulance stood empty, its doors still open. People clustered around the entrance to the building. Mrs. Norlund, holding Rachel's head to her, a hand covering her face, walked quickly with her past television cameras and whirring and clicking cameras and faces shouting questions.

Several nurses seemed to have been waiting for her. One came forward quickly and, smiling, touched her hair and said you just come with me, dear.

"Where's my mother?"

"They're taking care of her." She led her into an examination room as Mrs. Norlund waited in the corridor, staring after her.

"Where's"—Rachel's chest kept heaving—"my mother?"

"They're taking care of her, they're doing everything for her."

Another woman, wearing a lab coat, came in. She said brightly, "Hi, Rachel. I'm Dr. McKenna."

"My mother." She felt like she was choking.

"They've taken her to the operating room. We'll let you know the minute we hear anything. I promise you."

Now would you sit up here for me, she asked. That's right, that's good. So tell me, dear, did he hurt you, say punch you, do anything? He pulled your hair? Anything else? You sure? Good, good. What do you feel, does anything hurt, what happens when I do this? Good. Now let's listen to your chest. Good, real good. And let's look at your eyes—look over here, up here. Good, real good. Now let's put this on—did you ever have your blood pressure taken before?

Later, an older doctor, a man who said he was a psychiatrist, came in and sat down with her and asked many of the same questions and then said you're some brave young lady. And after he left Dr. McKenna said they wanted her to rest for a while.

"I don't want to."

"You'll see. Just in this room over here."

A nurse took her in, and she lay down, still in her camp clothes except for her sneakers. The nurse tucked a blanket around her, though she didn't want it; but the nurse seemed to know something about her that she didn't know, for she immediately began to shiver. But it passed in a couple of minutes, and the nurse seemed to know that too. She left, and Mrs. Norlund appeared in the doorway. Mrs. Norlund sat next to her in a white plastic chair.

No, not yet, sweetheart. "We'll be hearing soon. Why don't you close your eyes?"

She shook her head quickly against the pillow, though she'd become very tired.

A nurse came in and felt her pulse. Much later Dr. McKenna came in.

"We just heard from the operating room. It's going well—she

should be in the recovery room soon. She was shot in the chest, but she's very, very fortunate. It penetrated the lung, but it didn't do anywhere near the kind of damage it could have."

"Oh, thank God," Mrs. Norlund said.

Rachel looked at them. She wanted to hear it again.

"She's doing very well," the doctor said. "Now you, young lady, have to get some sleep."

No, they didn't see any reason why she had to stay here, she said to Mrs. Norlund.

"You'll come home with me," Mrs. Norlund said.

But she didn't want that. She'd stay at Tiffany's or Tracy's—

A sudden thought jolted her.

How could she face Tiffany, Tracy—any of the kids—again? With what they knew about her Mom.

And what she knew about her Mom. . . .


LYNN KEPT WAKING and drifting back to sleep the next morning and was about to slip off again when she saw, hazily, that the two figures in her room were not doctors or nurses this time. Rachel and Mrs. Norlund, who'd been watching her from the foot of the bed, approached her, Rachel a little hesitantly. Lynn started to reach out to Rachel, but it was the arm with the IV, and she held out her other hand and touched her cheek. Mrs. Norlund, leaning forward briefly, squeezed her forearm, then walked out and closed the door.

She looked at Rachel, her eyes filling. "You—okay?"

Rachel nodded.

"Where did you stay?"

"Mrs. Norlund's."

"She's—so nice."

Rachel looked at her. She didn't seem to know what to say. "What did they do to you?"

"Oh—they put a tube here." She touched her chest. "Some air came out, and this will help expand it."

"Will you always have to have it?"

"No."

Rachel nodded again. She looked at the IV needle, then up the tubing; she didn't seem to know where to look.

233

"Rach?"

Rachel looked back at her.

"I'm sorry." Tears began streaming down.

Rachel acted as though she didn't know what she meant. She shrugged slightly.

"I'm sorry. I'm so sorry."

Rachel frowned. For the first time her face showed some expression.

"Rach, I love you."

There was a sudden glisten of tears. "I love you too."

"Oh, Rach." She touched her cheek again, and Rachel bent over and they kissed. Lynn held on tightly, then released her, but kept holding her hand.

"I've put you through such hell," and she tightened her hand briefly. She could feel herself beginning to drift off again, and tried not to. But she opened her eyes after what seemed like a second to see Rachel and Mrs. Norlund sitting across from her, and Glenn standing by the door. Mrs. Norlund, standing up hesitantly, said, "Rachel didn't want to leave until you woke up."

Lynn held out her hand to Mrs. Norlund. "What can I say? How can I begin?"

"You don't have to say anything."

"Thank you hardly seems enough, but—thank you." Lynn lifted up slightly to kiss her. "Thank you so much." She turned to Rachel. "Sweetheart, you go. I'll call you, or you call here."

Rachel nodded.

"Are you going to Tiffany's?"

Rachel shrugged. "I don't know."

Mrs. Norlund spoke up. "She and I are going to have ourselves a good time. We're going to take rides, we'll—In fact, my sister-in-law has a place at a beautiful little lake. I'll talk to her, and if Rachel wants to we'll spend a few days there."

Lynn said, "That sounds wonderful," but she understood, and felt the start of tears again. "Sweetheart, I'll talk to you a little later."

Rachel leaned over and they kissed. She straightened up slowly. She seemed reluctant to leave. Hesitantly, "You going to be all better?"

"Of course I will."

234

Rachel nodded. Lynn could see her swallow.

Lynn watched her walk off, then turned her face away from Glenn. Why hadn't she died? Why hadn't she died like she wanted to?

She said, without looking at him, "I've really fixed her. Jon fixed her, and now I've fixed her."

"Well—you must have done something right. I spent some time with her at the house this morning. She's a remarkable young lady."

He came over and stood next to her. She said, still without turning to him, "Why don't I scream? They must be giving me something. I should be lying here screaming. I should be running down the hall screaming."

She felt his hand take hers. He said, "You should be happy. She got out of there alive, you got out of there. You should be proud of yourself."

She looked at him, her eyes watering over. "I'm not proud of myself. How can I be proud of myself?" Then she said quietly, "I just remembered—I told her I'd call her. The phone's off. I hear every reporter's been calling and trying to come up here."

"I'll tell her."

"They must be after her."

"Oh—just leave it to my mother."

She looked away from him again, across her shoulder. "You have a scoop, you know. An exclusive."

He turned her face back, gently, and kissed her lightly on the lips. He kept stroking the hair back from her forehead. "Really? About what?"

FROM THE DOORWAY Lynn watched as her doctor stood outside a room down the corridor, reading a chart before entering. You're doing fine, just fine, he'd said; should be going home in a few more days.

She lingered there a while, wondering should she take a little walk—you should walk more, he'd said—but went over to the chair by her window and sat down with one of the magazines on the windowsill. But she put it aside—she just couldn't keep her mind on it.

She should be happy she was leaving, and was, she thought; but

235

it was frightening too. She was so insulated here. The doctors, the nurses, everyone—they were all so nice, though for the first couple of days, probably, more of them than had to had come in for some reason or other. And she hadn't looked at a newspaper or newscast.

"Hi."

She looked at the doorway quickly. It was Manya with her high-coiled blonde hair, in lemon slacks and ruffled blouse, holding a box of candy.

"Honey, it's so good to see you sitting up. You look mar-ve-lous." She came over and kissed her and set down the candy. Then she stepped back a little, looking at her. "You look marvelous. Beautiful as ever. I'm so happy. I was afraid."

"I'm so glad to see you. Bring that chair over."

"No, no, I'm going to be leaving. I just wanted to see you. Sam's waiting. He's got one of those *deals*. I'm getting tired of *deals*."

"Just a little while if you can." Manya, she sensed, was uneasy about staying. After all, they'd never so much as shopped together. "Please. I'm so glad to see you."

"Well, just a little." She brought over a chair and sat on the edge. "You look so good. How do you feel?"

"Okay. They tell me I can go home in a few days."

"Good. Oh, I'm so happy . . . What you've been through. Sam and I, that's all we talk about. There's such nuts in this world—in everything. They're just waiting to go off—it could be getting the wrong chopped liver. But we've decided—Sam, me, my daughter, my son-in-law—I'm not going to work there any more. I'm going to do it from home. Nobody knows your number, just the office's. And you know what you save on the car?"

Lynn looked at her as she nodded to herself. Somehow, the few times she thought of that place, she pictured it closed. . .

"So tell me about you, your daughter. That poor child. I never met her, but I feel I know her. How is she?"

"She seems—you know, all right, but I don't know. We'll see. I've screwed her up good."

Manya looked at her with a pinch of a frown.

"And I've got to keep myself from being a mental case. A shrink

236

here says I should think about seeing a shrink. You name it, I feel guilty about it . . . Everything . . . Him."

Manya didn't seem to understand. Then, "*Him?* That crazy? That *meshugener?* Almost killed you? Rachel?"

"I do."

"Hon-ey," she admonished. "Hon-ey. You're just feeling very low. And it's natural. You've really been through it. Shrink, you're not going to need a shrink. I don't know you long, but I know you."

"You know, before you got here I was sitting here thinking— I'm afraid to leave."

"You mean people?"

"People. I don't know what-all. Oh, I'll be all right. I think basically I'm pretty strong. I guess—I know—my biggest concern is Rachel."

"Rachel, what? What about Rachel? You're afraid you've lost her? She doesn't like you any more? Hates you?"

"Maybe. That. And what this'll do to her."

"How old's she? Twelve?"

"Yes."

"Honey, let me tell you what I think. I've got a daughter, which makes me half an authority. The only way you're going to lose her is to being a teenager. And from what I hear, it's bad if you don't. But let me tell you something. They come back, the sons of bitches."

Lynn smiled. "Manya, that's terrible."

"It's true. And let me tell you what else I think. She's hurt, she's suffered, she'll suffer. God knows, we don't want our kids to hurt. But let me tell you—it may not be bad in the long run to know she's got a mother who knows how to say shit instead of do-do."

"Come on." But she was still smiling.

"I mean it. And you, as for you, you think you're strong? I really believe that if you think you're strong, you are strong. So I put my money on you. As for friends, lovers, you-name-it—kiddo, whoever you lose, you never really had. If you never heard that one before, I'll take credit for it."

Lynn looked at her. She wanted to put her arms around her.

"You're going to do fine, honey," Manya said. "You listen to me." She slapped her thighs. "Look, I got Sam."

"Manya, let's stay in touch."

Manya looked at her, a little surprised. "I'd like that. But Sam'll talk your ears off."

Lynn laughed and stood up with her. "Manya, thanks so much." "For what?"

Lynn embraced her, held her hard. Then she walked her to the doorway.

Manya said, "Remember what I said. You're going to do fine, Rachel will do fine, everything's going to work out for you. Okay?"

"Okay."

"Take care." Manya waved and walked off.

Lynn watched her. She felt a swelling in her chest, a feeling of joy that radiated and tingled through her. She kept looking long after Manya turned the corner.

Oh Manya. You do tell the truth too, don't you?